THICK GIRLS TAKE CHANCES

PEACHES & POLE

TINA GALLAGHER

Thick Girls Take Second Chances

By: Tina Gallagher

Published by Galsalla Press

Copyright © 2024

Cover Design: Qamber Designs & Emporium

Editor: Jeannine Luby

THICK GIRLS TAKE CHANCES

TINA GALLAGHER

CHAPTER 1

Eve

I STARED AT THE BLINKING CURSOR, PRAYING FOR DIVINE intervention to drop words into my head. Obviously not just any words. Wonderful words. Magical words. Or at least words my readers won't give a one-star review.

My cell vibrated, giving me a reason to tear my eyes away from the blank page. I smiled as my favorite aunt's face filled the screen.

"Aunt Winnie. How was the yoga retreat?"

"It was wonderful. The villa was absolutely beautiful and I felt such an amazing connection to all the attendees."

"I'm glad you enjoyed yourself."

"I truly did. There's nothing like getting away from your normal space. It really helps recenter and rejuvenate," she said.

"Your normal space is pretty great, but I suppose it still doesn't compare to Tuscany."

"Seaside is lovely but it's nice to visit other parts of the world from time to time. There's a different energy everywhere and it's so healthy to experience and absorb it."

Aunt Winnie is what my grandmother called *a hippy-dippy*. After graduating high school, she hopped into a Volkswagen Vanagon with five other people, hit the road, and lived like a nomad. She eventually settled in the idyllic town of Seaside, Oregon. And despite the fact she lived across the country from me, we managed to form a deep bond through her annual visits, phone calls, and a lot of letters.

"I should join you next time. A yoga retreat in Tuscany may be what I need to get myself straightened out."

"Oh honey, are you still having trouble writing?"

I nodded, even though she can't see.

"I've been a writer for the better part of a decade and yet, for the past three years, the words just won't come. It's like I forgot how to write. What's wrong with me?"

"You've experienced trauma and need to give yourself time to heal from that."

"The divorce was final three years ago. I should be healed by now."

"Hmmm, maybe," she said. "If you actually dealt with what happened."

"I think I dealt with it pretty well. As soon as I found out John was cheating, I told him I wanted a divorce. I even went back to using my maiden name once it was final. Not to mention how I stepped out of my comfort zone and started taking pole dance fitness classes. I'm in better shape than I was at eighteen. Plus, I've made some amazing friends."

"That's all wonderful dear, but it doesn't mean you've mentally sorted through it all or let it go," she pointed out. "And the divorce isn't the only trauma you've experienced. Grace graduated college then moved to England to pursue her master's degree. That's a big change for a parent."

"I agree, the divorce and Grace moving across the pond were both big changes. But I honestly don't think either of those are my issue."

"Then what is?"

"I wish I knew."

Thankfully I had some books stockpiled so my publishing schedule hasn't totally

stopped, just slowed down a bit. But the last of my reserves is releasing next month, so if I don't write something else soon, I don't know what I'll do.

"I have an idea," Aunt Winnie said. "Why don't you come here for an extended visit?"

"I appreciate that, but I don't think I can."

"Why on Earth not?"

"I really need to get at least one book done and I don't write well on vacation."

"Everly, you haven't written well for the past three years and you haven't gone anywhere."

"Uh oh, using my full name. You must be serious."

"I am serious," she said. "A change of scenery might be just what you need. Plan on staying for the summer."

Honestly, there's no reason for me not to go. The only thing I'll be leaving behind is pole class. I'll miss my pole peeps, but it's only for a few months. If there's a chance it will help my words flow again, I'll take it. Plus, it will be good to visit Aunt Winnie. We haven't seen each other in person since Grace's college graduation last year.

"Thanks Aunt Winnie. I'll book a flight and let you know when I'll be there."

MAX

. . .

"Let me help you with that, Pop," I said. "Why didn't you wait for me?"

"I'm not an invalid. I've been unloading my own truck since before you were born."

Which is exactly why he shouldn't be doing it by himself. Instead of saying that and starting an argument, I emptied the last few items out of the truck. I watched my grandfather limp around to the passenger side and pull his toolbox out of the back seat.

"I can handle this if your gout is acting up."

"I'm fine," he grumbled. "Besides, this is a two-man job."

"It'll be easier with two, but I can handle it on my own if you need to rest."

"Ach, I'll rest when I'm dead."

It seems like he's pretty grumpy this morning so I let the subject drop. The man is seventy-four years old. He's not going to change his ways at this point.

I grabbed a hammer and pry bar out of my toolbox and walked over to start the demo. The small deck we're replacing is in pretty bad shape, so it didn't take too long to dismantle.

Pop stood off to the side and watched as I knocked down the rest of the deck. His foot must really be bothering him because he's never one to just observe, he's usually right in the action showing me how to do it the "right way."

Once I had the whole thing torn apart, I tossed the old wood into the bed of my pickup and joined Pop over by the pile of new material.

"I hope this scheme of yours works. Otherwise, we're gonna be in the hole on this job. My quotes don't leave enough room for us to spend double on material."

We usually cut all the material on site, but I suggested we start doing at least some of it in Pop's workshop and bring it with us instead. This is a small project, so it seemed like a good one to try my way. Surprisingly, he agreed without too much complaint.

"If it doesn't work, I'll pay for new material out of my own pocket."

"I forgot you have those Hollywood big bucks and don't have to worry about sticking to a budget."

Ignoring the jab, I picked up my toolbelt and snapped it into place. Pop generally isn't a ray of sunshine, but he's usually in a better mood than this. The best thing I can do is get to work and finish this job early so he can go home and rest.

We worked side by side and got the flooring and steps done in record time. Thankfully all the cut pieces fit with minimal tweaking.

"Let's take a break," I said. "I'm starving."

One thing I've learned through the years working with Pop is that he'll keep going until a job is done. But if I stop, he'll stop. So I make it a point to at least break for a drink to ensure he stays hydrated.

I ran to my truck and grabbed the cooler out of the back seat and joined Pop on the newly-constructed steps. Reaching inside, I handed him a bottle of water and a ham and cheese sandwich.

"Winnie Everly called last night. Her porch steps are loose and she needs a window in her studio replaced. Do you think you can handle that Saturday?"

That could explain some of his mood today, too. He and Winnie have been circling around each other since I moved here twelve years ago, and probably a couple decades before that too. I have no idea why they don't just get together. They're not getting any younger.

"Sure."

"I'd do it myself, but I have that meeting with the festival planning committee." He took a bite of his sandwich and chewed. "That shouldn't take too long though so maybe I can take care of Winnie's projects in the afternoon instead of having you do it."

"I don't have any plans for Saturday, so it's no problem."

"Guess I better take you up on that now because once the festival starts, you'll probably be busy." He grunted and shook his head. "You're thirty-four. Time to start settling down instead of just fooling around, don't you think?"

I'll admit that for the first few years I lived here, I was *very busy* during festival season. Vacationing women were perfect for what I was looking for at the time. Namely no-strings sex and for them to leave when it was over. And even though I haven't done that in a long time, Pop still brings it up every year.

The truth is, I'd settle down tomorrow if I found the right woman, but no one in Seaside fits that description. Maybe someday.

CHAPTER 2

Eve

"I can't believe you're leaving us."

Anjannette draped her arms around my shoulders and pulled me in for a dramatic hug as she said those words.

"I'm only going for the summer."

She pulled away to look me in the eye.

"That's too long. I'll miss you."

"And we all know you're going to go out there, fall in love with the town handyman, and stay in Seaside forever," Keera said.

"That only happens in Hallmark Channel movies. My life isn't that romantic. Never was." I shook my head. "Writers are told to write what they know. I don't know what ever possessed me to write romance."

"Well, you're very good at it so there must have been some romance in your life at some point," Anjannette said. "Even with my shitty exes there were a few decent moments."

"John and I started dating in college so having a pizza date before sex instead of getting a booty call at midnight was considered romantic."

That led to a whole conversation about pathetic pick-up lines and bad decisions. Although Anjannette and Keera have both recently found happiness with amazing men, they had tons of stories from their dating days. Sophie is the opposite. Like me, she married young and divorced a couple decades later. Unlike me, there was no infidelity involved in the breakup. She and her husband just drifted apart and decided to call it quits. So, the stories she's sharing are all recent as she jumped back into the dating scene with both feet in the last year.

Sad to say, I don't have anything to add to the conversation. Other than John, I only had a few boyfriends in high school. They all know what happened with the former and there's not much to tell with the latter.

"I honestly don't know how I wrote anything interesting before I met you ladies. My life is so boring compared to yours," I said. "You don't have to worry about me never coming back. I need your stories for inspiration. That is, if I ever start writing again."

"You'll get there. You have to." Keera pointed at me then Sophie. "Now that you got me hooked on the genre, you two better never stop writing it."

"I'm going to Seaside to hopefully get the creative juices flowing again."

"Maybe some other juices will flow while you're there too," Sophie bobbed her eyebrows. "It might not end like a sappy TV movie, but I'm sure there's a sexy handyman or veterinarian who'd be up for a summer fling."

"That's not on my agenda. I'm going to spend time with my aunt and focus on writing."

"Not for nothing, maybe a good fuck is just what you need," Keera said. "It might inspire you."

"I'm not really ready for that. Or maybe I'm just scared." I shook my head. "I don't know, but the thought of having sex with someone besides John freaks me out. I mean, there are men I find attractive, but I don't feel that *need* or *desire* like I had way back when with John."

"My first time post-divorce was weird, but it wasn't bad," Sophie said. "Maybe you just need to fake it 'til you make it. You know, find a guy and just do it. The first time is always the hardest. After that, it's smooth sailing."

"You at least had a college experience or two before you got married. John *was* my college experience. Before him, I'd barely seen a penis, much less touched one." I rested my head in my hands. "I'm forty-two and I've only had sex with one man. I'm basically a unicorn."

No one commented on that and I looked up to find three sets of bewildered eyes staring at me.

"Oh God, I've stunned you into silence."

"It's not that," Anjannette said. "Your life is just so different from mine so I'm trying to put myself in your shoes. Honestly, I could see myself feeling the same way you do." She put her arm around my shoulders and squeezed. "Just make sure that if the opportunity does present itself, you'll at least consider climbing some hot handyman like a tree."

I burst out laughing. Her tone was so serious then she ended with that.

"I promise."

MAX

. . .

THE WAITRESS PLUNKED DOWN TWO PINTS AND AN ORDER OF loaded nachos. Once she left, I picked up my beer and held it up.

"To your first night out in nearly a year. Enjoy."

I tapped my glass against my friend Dex's, then took a long drink before setting it down.

"It's only been nine months, but thanks."

For the first time in a long time, Dex and I are hanging out at The Rusty Skipper. We used to come here a couple times a week, but since he got married, that dwindled down to maybe once a month. And it hasn't happened at all since the twins were born.

"So, what's it like without Courtney and the twins home?"

"Quiet. Sometimes too quiet," Dex said. "I think I've gotten used to the chaos and don't know how to function without it."

"I'll be honest, I never thought you'd settle down."

"Me neither." He shook his head. "Then Courtney came to town and that was it."

Dexter Doyle is my best friend and was my one-time wing man on the Seaside dating scene. But he fell head over heels in love with a woman who came here on vacation a few years ago. They did the long-distance thing for a little while, then he somehow convinced her to move here permanently. They married three years ago and the twins, Andrew and Aaron, came last October. It's been interesting watching him transform into a married man and father.

"So how long is she visiting her parents?"

"A week. She's only been gone two days and it seems like forever."

"That's love."

His eyes widened.

"I never thought I'd ever hear you say something so sappy."

I didn't know what to say to that, so I just shrugged and perused the mound of nachos. After finding one perfectly piled with meat, cheese, salsa, and a single jalapeno, I picked it up and popped it into my mouth.

"Have you been seeing anyone lately?" he asked when it was obvious I wasn't going to say more.

"No, not in a while," I said. "You know what it's like here."

I dated a couple women who lived in town when I was in my early twenties, but that got messy a few times when they wanted more and I didn't. So I started focusing on the ones who were just visiting, especially the festival goers. They were usually just up for a fun, uncomplicated, fling. But at some point, that got monotonous.

"Hey, all the other guys got married and I found Courtney. You never know who's going to pop into town and change your life."

Through the years, our whole friend group got married. Dex and I were the last singletons, and now it's just me. And it seems that anytime I see my old friends, instead of wanting to hang out, they try to set me up with someone.

"What is it with you married people always trying to get the rest of us hitched?"

"Hey, when you find something good, you share it with your friends." He laughed then finished his beer in one long gulp. "Are you having another one?"

"Just one more," I said. "I'm fixing a couple things at Winnie Everly's tomorrow and I want to get an early start so I finish before Pop shows up."

"I'm surprised he's not going there himself."

He waggled his eyebrows.

"He has a meeting with the festival committee in the morning. After he asked me if I could go, he said he could make it in the afternoon, but his gout has been acting up so I want him to take a break."

"Good luck with that."

"Thanks, I'll definitely need it."

CHAPTER 3

Eve

"Y{sc}OU FINALLY MADE IT.}"

Aunt Winnie engulfed me in a big hug. I swear we were the same height at one point, but for the past few years I have to bend slightly to accept her embrace. But everything else about her is the same. Braided hair hanging to the middle of her back, flowy boho dress, and lingering scent of patchouli define her as much as her well-worn Birkenstocks, silver bangles, and turquoise rings.

"It's so good to see you." I pulled back to look at her beautiful face. "When my flights kept getting postponed, I thought I was going to end up sleeping at the airport."

She shifted but kept her arm around my waist, leading me toward baggage claim.

"You poor thing, you look exhausted."

"I was afraid I was going to oversleep and miss my flight, so I didn't sleep well. And for whatever reason, sitting around the airport for hours is exhausting."

We lined up at the baggage claim carousel with the other passengers.

"Besides being tired, you're probably starving. I didn't plan dinner because I figured we'd go out, so we'll just grab some takeout on the way home. You can eat, decompress a little, then get to sleep."

"Add a shower to that list and it sounds like a perfect night."

Aunt Winnie nodded then shifted her attention to the carousel as it started moving.

"How many bags do you have?"

"Just one."

"*One*? For the whole summer?"

"It's really big." I nodded toward the laptop case hanging from my left shoulder. "And I have some things in here just in case they lose my luggage."

Thankfully that last thing didn't happen. I breathed a sigh of relief when I spotted my orange suitcase. I stepped up and grabbed it, then moved back next to Aunt Winnie. After pulling the handle up and sliding my laptop case over it, we were on our way to the parking lot.

"I can't believe you still have Gertrude," I said, referring to the yellow Volkswagen Beetle she's been driving as long as I can remember.

"Gertrude and I have been together a long time. Anytime I think about trading her in for something with all the bells and whistles, I feel guilty."

She unlocked the doors the old-fashioned way and I placed my bags in the back before climbing into the passenger seat. Aunt Winnie got behind the wheel and with the turn of the key, the engine purred to life and we were off.

I was too exhausted to appreciate the scenery during the short ride but consoled myself with the fact that I'd have the whole summer to enjoy it. After a quick stop at Mo's Seafood & Chowder to pick up dinner, we pulled into Aunt Winnie's driveway.

I got out of the car and opened the back passenger-side door to retrieve my bags.

"I was expecting you tomorrow."

Aunt Winnie's words confused me until I saw an older gentleman walk toward us from the back of the house. I slammed the door shut and missed the first words he spoke, but heard the last few.

"I'm just checking the measurements for your steps."

He glanced at the small notebook in his hand then tucked it into his back pocket.

"Henry, this is my niece Eve Reese. She's staying with me for the summer." Aunt Winnie looked at me. "Eve, Henry Corbin is the town handyman. I'm having the back porch steps replaced and a window in my studio fixed."

I smothered my smirk as I said hello to Henry. My pole peeps will be disappointed to hear the town handyman would be a better love match for Aunt Winnie than me. Not that I'm surprised. Like I told them, my life isn't that romantic.

MAX

I SLAMMED THE TAILGATE CLOSED WITH MORE FORCE THAN necessary. It's been a clusterfuck of a morning and I needed some way to vent my frustration. Childish? Maybe. But as I got behind the wheel, I have to admit it helped a little.

My plan was to get to Winnie's at six, but the clock just

hit seven-thirty, and I'm not even at her place yet. I overslept this morning, which is part of the reason I'm running late, but that's not totally to blame. The lumberyard lost my order so instead of just doing a quick pick up, I helped the staff put it together. To make things worse, they didn't have the window size I needed, so I had to drive a half hour to their other store location to grab it.

Now I'm back on the highway. If all goes well, I should still be able to finish by the time Pop shows up.

Winnie's yellow Beetle wasn't in the driveway when I arrived, which is probably the best thing that's happened so far today. She's truly one of my favorite people in Seaside, but I just want to get to work without having to exchange pleasantries. I'm already too far behind.

I finished my second coffee of the morning and got out of the truck. After grabbing my tools from the back seat, I put on a 90's playlist, and got to work removing boards.

I'm just replacing the steps, but I checked the structure of the rest of the porch to be sure it's sound. Pop said he did it, but I wouldn't put it past him to purposely overlook something just to see if I'd notice. He used to do stuff like that when I first started working with him and still surprises me once in a while just to make sure I'm paying attention.

Thankfully everything looks good and after double-checking Pop's measurements, I got to work cutting boards.

CHAPTER 4

Eve

I drifted in that space between sleep and wakefulness, "Wonderwall" by Oasis playing in my head. Refusing to open my eyes, I burrowed down into the covers and smiled as "Rain King" by Counting Crows started to play. It's one of my favorite songs and I haven't heard it in forever.

Floating in and out of semi-consciousness, I snuggled into the comfortable bed and enjoyed my mental playlist. It's been a long time since I allowed myself to sleep in, but yesterday was a long day and I'm in no hurry to fully wake. I took in a long deep breath and slowly let it out as I was serenaded back to sleep by U2.

A high-pitched whining broke my peaceful slumber and I put the pillow over my head to tune it out. It stopped, then sounded again in short bursts a few more times. Then the banging started. I grasped my head with both hands and moaned, then sat up and whipped the covers off.

Swinging my legs over the side of the bed, I cringed

when the noise started again. There's no way I'm going to get back to sleep so I stood and headed to the bathroom. After taking care of business, I studied my reflection in the mirror while I brushed my teeth. It's not good.

Some people travel well. I am not one of those people. I usually look like crap after flying and this time is no different. The circles under my eyes look even darker on my paler-than-usual face and it's going to take me forever to detangle my hair.

I rinsed and spit, grateful that at least my mouth feels better. The only thing that will fix my hair is a good washing with tons of conditioner, so I ran a brush through it to get some of the knots out and pulled it into a messy bun. It's not great, but what does it matter? Like Alexis Rose says in *Schitt's Creek*, "No one cares, David."

I peeked out the bathroom window before heading downstairs. Aunt Winnie's car isn't in the driveway, so I guess it's only me here. Well, me and whoever is making all the racket outside.

The noise got louder as I made my way downstairs. In fact, it sounded like it was right outside the kitchen door. A peek through the curtains explained why that was so. It *was* right outside the kitchen door. Without thinking, I pulled the door open and stepped onto the porch.

"*What* are you doing?"

The hammering stopped and my heart followed suit when the person responsible for the noise looked up. Chocolate brown eyes met mine and after its initial stall, my heart pounded at an alarming rate.

Holy shit.

I took long, slow breaths in an effort to control my heartbeat. Talk about an inopportune time for my libido to come to life.

His eyes took a lazy tour of my body. It was then I realized I was only dressed in a pink nightshirt that stopped at mid-thigh. To cover my embarrassment, I lashed out.

"Do you know what time it is?"

The man lifted his left hand and glanced at his watch.

"Eight thirty."

"It's Saturday morning."

The corner of his mouth kicked up into an adorable smile as he dragged his fingers through his thick black hair.

"That it is."

"What are you doing?" I asked again, then felt silly because it's pretty obvious. Still, he played along and answered anyway.

"Replacing the steps. Once I'm done here, I'll change out that window in Winnie's studio."

He pointed across the yard to the item in question.

"This early?"

He chuckled.

"I guess your nightie doesn't lie."

I glanced down at my nightshirt and its picture of Grumpy proclaiming, "I Don't Do Mornings" and crossed my arms over my chest.

"I'm sorry, I had a hellish travel day yesterday. Aunt Winnie didn't tell me someone was going to be hammering outside my bedroom window this morning."

"Then I'm glad I overslept and didn't get here at six like I'd originally planned."

"I'm glad too," I said. "Although I was enjoying your music."

"Yeah, it's a good playlist." He tapped his hammer against his thigh. "I'm Max, by the way."

"Eve."

I leaned forward and shook his proffered hand. My eyes

rounded at the zing that radiated up my arm but instead of letting go like I should have, I held on longer than is socially acceptable.

"So, you're Winnie's niece."

He raised his voice slightly on the last word turning his sentence into a question. I dropped his hand and took a big step back.

"Yes, I'm here visiting for the summer." I shifted my eyes toward the two new steps then back at Max. "I thought Henry was the only handyman in town."

"He is. I mean, we work together. Well, I work for him. He's my grandfather."

I nodded, mesmerized by his eyes. There's also something else, a connection. I feel like I know him from somewhere. Shaking my head to rid it of that thought, I cleared my throat.

"Well I uh–I better let you get back to work."

Our eyes held as I backed up and stepped over the threshold. Before I closed the door, Max said, "I'll see you around, Eve."

It's been a long time, but I know when I'm being flirted with. I just don't remember how to respond. So instead of saying anything, I let out a small squeak, slammed the door, and ran up to my room.

MAX

I STARED AT THE CLOSED DOOR FOR AN EMBARRASSINGLY LONG time after Eve went back inside. Realizing what I was doing, I shook my head and got back to work. I really want to finish before Pop shows up. I can't waste time daydreaming about the woman I just met. There'll be time for that later.

These steps are going to be the easy part of this job. The window will be the challenge. The building Winnie uses as her studio is an old carriage barn that was built before levels, rulers, or right angles were used. I helped Pop replace the front door a few years ago and it was a bitch. I'm expecting nothing less with the window.

I set the next step and hammered it into place, then did the same with the remaining two. With that done, I headed back to my truck for a drink. I grabbed a bottle of water out of the cooler then leaned against the tailgate and downed half its contents with one long chug.

Out of the corner of my eye, I saw something in the second-floor window and looked up. A blur of pink was all I saw before the curtain fell back into place. I kept my eyes trained on that spot as I finished the rest of the water, but Eve never appeared again. Still, it's nice to think that maybe she was watching me.

I crushed the water bottle and tossed it back in the cooler. Grabbing my Bluetooth speaker and tools, I headed across the yard to the studio to get to work. I'd just finished removing putty and inside vertical strips from the window when I heard Winnie pulling up the driveway. I waved just as she stepped out of the car.

"Hi Max," she said as she opened the trunk, which was full of bags.

"Let me help you with those," I said as I walked toward her.

"Thank you." She picked up two bags and stepped aside. "I haven't had a grocery order this big in a long time, but my niece is visiting."

Grabbing the rest of the bags, I followed Winnie to the porch.

"Yeah, Eve and I met."

She glanced over her shoulder and smiled. I thought she was going to say something about Eve, but instead she complimented the steps.

"They look wonderful."

"Thank you." I followed her inside and set the bags down on the kitchen table. "Pop didn't say anything about staining them. Did you want that done, too?"

"I'd like the whole porch stained, but that can wait until you're less busy. The important thing is that the steps are fixed. I've been putting it off for a while and they were getting pretty bad." She put milk and eggs in the refrigerator then turned to face me. "So you met Eve?"

It took me a second to catch up with the change of topic, but once I did, I nodded.

"She's staying for the summer."

"Yeah, she mentioned that."

"She hasn't visited here in years. Maybe you can show her around sometime."

If I'm reading the room right, Winnie is playing matchmaker. Normally I hate that kind of thing, but I have to say, I'm not opposed.

Last night, Dex said he thinks I'm in a rut. I don't think my life is in such a sad shape, but it's definitely become routine over the past couple years. Maybe the woman whose touch made my palm tingle is just the person to shake things up a bit.

CHAPTER 5

Eve

My phone buzzed, pulling my attention from the blank page. I smiled when I saw my daughter's face on the screen.

"Finally. We've been playing phone tag for two days."

"Sorry, I've been swamped," Grace said.

"How are you? Did you get all your papers written?"

"I handed the last one in yesterday. And to celebrate, I'm heading to London for the weekend with some friends."

"That's great. I know you're there to get a master's degree, but I want you to enjoy your experience at Cambridge, too."

"I am. What about you? Are you having fun with Aunt Winnie?"

"For sure. You know how amazing she is and it's so beautiful here." I sighed. "I wish I visited more through the years. Instead, we only saw each other during her annual trips to Scranton."

"Well, you're there now and that's all that matters. In

fact, once you're done there, you should come here for an extended stay. There's plenty of room in my flat. You've always wanted to live in England."

That's true. I planned on studying abroad when I was in college, but got pregnant before that happened. I've never regretted having my daughter, but there are things I wish I'd gotten to experience. So of course I've done my best to make sure Grace didn't miss out on anything without being too much of a nag.

"Thanks honey, but you don't want your mom there cramping your style."

"I could call you Eve and tell everyone you're my sister. God knows you look young enough."

"I appreciate that," I said. "Let's talk about it after I see how this summer goes."

"Don't think I'll forget about it." The line was quiet for a few seconds before Grace spoke again. "Mom, in between writing amazing books, make sure you enjoy your experience in Seaside. Relax, maybe hook up with a hot guy."

"*Grace!*"

I tried to sound shocked, but couldn't stop laughing.

"What? You're young and single," she said. "Live a little."

"I'll live once I finish my book."

That led to a conversation about my lack of writing, then the subject shifted to her classes and what she planned to do in London. When she yawned, I glanced at the clock on my nightstand. It's almost midnight in England.

"I'll let you get to sleep. I love you, honey. Enjoy London. Send pictures."

"I love you too," she said. "And I will. Tell Aunt Winnie hi and that I love her too."

I hung up and looked at my computer. I've been sitting here longer than I care to admit and once again, have nothing to show for it. Standing, I slipped on my sandals and headed downstairs. It's such a beautiful day and I've been cooped up inside. Maybe a walk on the beach will help clear my mind and the words will flow.

When I didn't find Aunt Winnie in the house, I walked out the backdoor to check in her studio. The window Max installed a few days ago was open and so was the front door. I knocked on the door jamb and she turned from the canvas in front of her.

"Come in." She gestured with a paintbrush. "How'd it go today?"

"Not well."

"Well, you just got here. Give it time."

I was going to say it's been almost three years, but don't want to whine about it anymore.

"I did talk to Grace though. She says to tell you hello and that she loves you."

"She's such a sweet girl," she said. "You did a good job raising her."

I smiled at her compliment and turned my attention to her painting.

"That's so beautiful." I looked around at all her finished works. "They all are. How is it

that you can create this, and I can't draw a straight line with a ruler?"

"We all have our own talents. You're an artist with words and I paint." She looked at the

work in front of her and frowned. "Of course, I don't paint faces. They never turn out quite the way I want them to."

The beach scene she's working on depicts a family having a picnic in the near distance, but none of the people's faces have features. Yet somehow, she manages to portray their happiness.

"What you do works." I studied the painting again, then turned to face her. "I'm going to take a walk on the beach and pray for inspiration."

Standing, she wrapped her arm around my shoulder and squeezed.

"The words will come. Just relax and enjoy being here." She pulled back to look me in the eye. "Maybe find a young man to spend time with. You do write romance after all. Having a romantic encounter might help with that."

That's the second time in ten minutes I've been told to find a man. Am I that pathetic?

"I don't know about that last thing, but I will relax and enjoy being here."

"You know, Max Corbin is single. And in case you didn't notice, he's good looking. He's also very sweet."

"I'd have to be dead to not notice Max's good looks, but I think he's a little young for me. How old is he anyway?"

"I have no idea," she said. "It doesn't matter anyway. Age is just a number."

"Aunt Winnie, I'm here to spend time with you and get my writing back on track, not have my own *How Stella Got Her Groove Back* experience."

"Who says you can't do all three?"

MAX

POP INVENTORIED OUR REMAINING SUPPLIES WHILE I SET THE batteries for our cordless tools into their chargers. We had a busy day building stages and structures at the festival grounds and tomorrow will be more of the same.

"This'll get us started tomorrow. We can figure out what else we need once we know exactly what we still have to do. They keep changing their minds."

What is usually a cookie-cutter job has turned into something a bit more complicated. The committee decided to change some things for this year's festival so we're playing it by ear.

"Sounds good," I said. "If there's nothing else to do down here, I'm going to take a shower to cool off."

"It was kinda warm today."

"That it was."

Plus, I worked double-time so Pop didn't have to walk around too much. His limp isn't as pronounced as it was a couple days ago, but I still don't want him to overdo it.

"No, we're done for the day," he said and I followed him to the door. "We'll have breakfast at the diner at six, then head over?"

"Sounds good."

That said, he walked across the yard to the house. I closed the workshop door and headed upstairs to my apartment. When I first moved here, I lived over there with him, but a few years later asked Pop if I could renovate the space above the workshop. I must have been getting on his nerves in the house because he immediately agreed. I could have bought my own place, but I like being close to Pop, just not under the same roof.

I stripped on my way to the bathroom, stepped into the shower, and turned on the water. A shiver ran through me as the cold spray hit my skin. Once I was sufficiently cooled off, I added some hot water to make the temperature more tolerable.

After washing off the dust of the day, I turned my back to the spray and let it loosen the muscles in my shoulders. I stood like that until my fingers turned pruney then I shut off the water, pulled a towel off the rack, and dried off.

I grabbed my cell on the way to the bedroom and saw a missed call from my mother. She didn't leave a message and I'm not going to call her back. Since I moved to Seaside twelve years ago, I've only spoken to her a handful of times and that was only when she wanted something. If it's really important, she'll leave a message.

Putting thoughts of my mother out of my mind, I slipped into a pair of shorts, grabbed a beer from the refrigerator, and headed onto the deck. Pop's property sits steps from the beach and the view is amazing, which is another reason I chose to stay here instead of buying my own place. I sat back in my Adirondack chair to enjoy it and my beverage.

I'd just finished my drink when the view got even better. I've been hoping I'd run into Eve again, and here she is walking right toward me. Setting the empty bottle down, I stood and made my way to the beach. Once I stepped onto the sand, I waved to catch her attention. Her eyes widened and she gave an awkward wave.

"It's nice to see you again, Eve."

"Hi Max."

"You remember my name."

"I never forget the names of people who wake me from a peaceful sleep with whining saws and pounding hammers."

"Sorry about that." I flashed a smile. "Don't worry, next time I'm working at Winnie's, I'll just be wielding a paint brush, so you'll be able to sleep soundly."

"Good to know." She looked over my head toward my deck. "That's your house?"

I nodded.

"I live above Pop's workshop. His house is right behind it. Well, right in front of it if you're coming from the road."

She nodded then looked out at the ocean.

"It's so beautiful here."

Without taking my eyes off her, I said, "It sure is."

Her eyes shifted back to mine and her cheeks seemed a little more pink than they had been a minute ago. I guess she caught my meaning. We stood just looking at each other for several heartbeats. My phone buzzed, breaking the spell. I slipped my hand in my pocket and silenced the call. Whoever it is can wait.

"Would you like to come up for a drink? The view is amazing from my deck."

"Oh thank you, but I uh, I better get back," she said.

I thought about trying to convince her, but would rather use my powers of persuasion for a real date.

"I'm actually glad I ran into you." She raised her right brow. "I was wondering if you'd like to go out to dinner this weekend."

"Oh thank you," she said as a way to turn me down for the second time in less than a minute. "But I really don't have time. I need to finish my book and I'm way behind."

"You need to take a break sometime and you have to eat." She shook her head and before she could say no again, I held out my hand. "I'll tell you what, I'll put my number in your phone and if it turns out you have some free time, text me and we'll go grab a bite to eat."

Her eyes shifted back and forth as she nibbled on her bottom lip. I thought she was going to refuse, but instead she pulled her phone out of her pocket and handed it to me. I took it and entered my number then gave it back to her.

"Text anytime," I said with a smile.

CHAPTER 6

Eve

Anjannette texted and asked if I'd want to do a Zoom happy hour. Of course I jumped at the invite. And even though it's only two-thirty here, I popped open a bottle of Merlot. Hey, it's after five back home. That counts, right?

"We miss you too," she said. "How's the writing?"

"Still nothing, but I sort of plotted the book, so I'll consider that progress."

"You plotted?" Sophie asked.

"I said 'sort of.'"

I don't normally plot my books. When I start writing, I know the beginning, black moment, and the end. I figure out the rest of the details as I go along.

Sophie is the opposite. She plans and outlines her books so as she writes, she knows exactly what's going to happen and when.

"What exactly did you do?"

"I wrote a short summary of what each chapter should be about. I'm sure it will change as I start writing, but at least it's a start." I shrugged. "Since my usual method of writing isn't working, I figured I'd try something new. I just did that today so I'll let you know if it works."

"You'll get it done," Sophie said with more confidence than I felt.

I've heard other authors complain about being blocked or burned out, but I've *never* had an issue so I'm in uncharted territory here.

"No more talk about writing or lack of," I said. "What's new with you guys?"

"Not much here," Keera said. "I'm just enjoying the summer and spending time with Simon."

"You guys are adorable together. I'm happy you finally noticed the man who was right under your nose for so many years."

"Yeah, me too," she said. "Now that we're together, I can't understand what took us so long. Well, what took *me* so long."

"You figured it out. That's all that matters."

"I told her I'm going to write a book about their story," Sophie said.

"It would make a great romance novel."

"If it gets made into a movie, I want Jennifer Aniston to play me," Keera said with a dramatic hair toss. Then she shifted her eyes toward Sophie. "You've got a little something going on that would make a good book."

"Let me refill before you start talking." I picked up the bottle, poured more wine into my glass, then held it in both hands. "Okay, I'm ready."

"I've been...*exploring* some things," Sophie said.

"*Things?*"

"I'm interested in learning more about BDSM, so I decided to go to a dungeon and check it out," she said. "I've only gone three times and right now I'm just watching. I'm not ready to participate yet. I don't know if I ever will be, but it's interesting."

I can't imagine diving into single life like Sophie has. She's out there dating and exploring. The most I've done is start taking pole dance lessons. But I'll admit, that has changed my life. It's made me more confident in my body plus I've made these amazing friends. So I won't beat myself up too much.

"Just take it one step at a time. You'll know if and when you're ready." Anjannette said.

"If nothing else, I can use what I learn in my books," Sophie said with a smile.

"You authors," Keera said. "Everything is research."

"You know it," I said then looked at Anjannette. "What have you been up to?"

"Some of Leo's family is visiting, so the house has been very crowded, but I'm having a good time. They've been keeping me occupied while he's on the road," Anjannette said. "Too bad you're across the country. Nicky was here for a couple days. You guys would get along well."

"Leo's brother is amazingly good-looking and charming, but he's also too young for me."

"Age is just a number," she said.

"You sound like Aunt Winnie."

The three of them perked up at that.

"What, or should I say *who*, did she say that about?" Anjannette asked as she tapped her

fingers against her wine glass.

"Was it a handyman or veterinarian?" Keera asked. My

face heated at her words. "Oh my God, there is someone. Tell us all the details."

I took a fortifying drink then set my wine glass down and held onto the stem.

"It's the handyman."

A mixture of cheers, shouts, and chuckles came through my speaker.

"Wait, I thought you said the handyman is Aunt Winnie's age." Sophie said then raised her brows. "Is that why she told you age is just a number?"

"God no," I said. "Henry is her age, but his grandson Max works with him."

"Oooh Max," Anjannette said, fluttering her eyebrows. "Tell us about him."

"Well he's incredibly hot and according to Aunt Winnie, single and sweet too."

"He sounds perfect!"

"He's also young."

"Define young," Keera said.

"I don't know exactly, but I'm guessing he's around your age."

"That's not too young," she said. "You're what forty?"

"Forty-two."

"You could definitely do him." Anjannette took a sip of wine, then added, "Or you know, ask him out."

"I've never asked a man out before. I wouldn't even know how."

"Are you interested in him?" Sophie asked.

I snorted as I topped off my glass again.

"I'd have to be dead not to be. The man is beautiful and he was barechested when I ran into him on the beach yesterday. It took all my willpower to not just stand there and stare." I picked up my glass but stopped just shy of my mouth. "And there's just something about him. We shook hands and–" I stopped speaking and took a drink.

"And what?" Keera asked. "Come on, you can't leave us hanging."

Three expectant faces stared back at me from the screen.

"I felt this zing." I rubbed at my palm as I remembered the feeling. "As soon as his hand touched mine, it was like I was holding a live wire."

"What more of a sign do you need?" Sophie asked. "Next time you see the man, ask him out."

My thoughts must have shown on my face and these women know me way too well not to read them.

"What's that look?" Anjannette asked.

"He may have already asked me out," I said. "And when I turned him down, he also may

have programmed his number into my phone so I could let him know if I change my mind."

I finished my wine in one long gulp.

"Pick up your phone and call the man," Keera said. I'm feeling a little fuzzy around the edges and her staccato tone made me giggle. "I'm serious. Do it now."

"Okay. Geez." I picked up my phone and brought up Max's number. "Do I have to call or do you think I can text him?"

They debated and discussed for what seemed like forever, but finally came to a unanimous decision.

"A text is fine," Anjannette said.

I typed and deleted three texts before the ladies and I were happy with the message. It's simple and to the point.

> Hi Max, it's Eve. I'd like to take you up on your offer of dinner if it still stands.

"You think that's good? Nothing else?"

"It's perfect," Sophie said.

Anjannette and Keera nodded in agreement.

My index finger hovered over the arrow and I took in a deep breath and let it out slowly before touching the screen, sending the text on its way.

"Done."

MAX

"I'M HAPPY YOU TEXTED," I SAID, FOR PROBABLY THE FIFTH time since I picked up Eve.

She looked up from the menu and smiled. I took it as a good sign that the expression on her face is less nervous than the one she wore earlier.

Instead of taking her to one of the establishments in Seaside, I decided to venture to a quaint Italian bistro Dex recommended about a half hour away. Aside from offering us some privacy from the peeping eyes of the town, the ride gave us time to chat and shake off some of the first-date jitters.

She glanced down at the menu then back at me.

"Have you been here before? What's good?"

"I haven't, but according to my friend Dex, you can't go wrong with anything on the menu. But, he also said that sometimes they have a pork ragu and parmesan over pappardelle pasta on special that he supposedly dreams about."

"Wow, that's a pretty solid recommendation."

"Dex takes his food seriously."

"Apparently."

The waitress approached to take our drink orders and also recited the specials. As soon as she mentioned the pork ragu, Eve glanced at me and smiled. A dimple popped out in her right cheek making her look even more adorable.

I don't know what it is about this woman, I feel something different with her. Granted, this is only the third time I've been in her presence, and the other times were short. But the feeling is there, warm and fuzzy deep inside. It's definitely something I'd like to explore.

"Well, I know what I'm having," I said when the waitress walked away.

"Me too."

She set her menu on the table and folded her hands in front of her.

"So how are you enjoying Seaside so far?"

"I haven't done much, other than the occasional walk on the beach," she said. "That's

something I definitely don't get to do at home, so it's been nice."

The waitress returned with our drinks and we gave our orders. Once she left, I picked up the conversation again.

"Where is home?"

"Pennsylvania. Scranton specifically."

"Scranton? Like *The Office?*"

"One and the same."

"That's pretty cool."

She shrugged.

"It's home."

"So what brought you here for the summer?"

"Aunt Winnie invited me."

Her blue eyes searched mine, as if she was trying to decide if she should reveal more. I must have passed some kind of test because she continued.

"I'm an author, but I've been having trouble writing. She thought the change of scenery would help."

"Has it?"

"Not yet."

"You've only been here a short time. Once Seaside soaks in, you'll be good." She crossed her index and middle fingers as she took a drink of water. "What do you write?"

"Romance novels."

That's not what I was expecting, but romance novels make up a huge chunk of the book market. Someone has to write them. Through appetizers and most of our main course, I asked about her career. How she got started. Where she comes up with story ideas. Who's her favorite character she's written.

She answered the last question but before I could ask another, held her hand up halting my words.

"Enough about me. Tell me about you."

"There's really not much to tell. I moved here about twelve years ago and started working with Pop."

"Where did you live before?"

"My mom moved to California when she was pregnant with me. She still lives there," I added before she had to ask.

"What made you move here?"

There's a lot that goes into that answer, but this is a first date, so I'll keep it light.

"I was looking for a change. Pop and I had mostly a long-distance relationship and I thought it was a good time to fix that."

"How old were you?"

"Twenty-two."

"So you're thirty-four?"

I nodded.

Her eyes shifted up and she shook her head.

"That's kind of what I thought, but I hoped I was wrong."

"Is that bad?"

"It's not great," she said around a chuckle.

"Why?"

"I'm forty-two."

I assumed she was around my age. Either way, I don't know why it matters and said so.

Eve placed her fork on her plate and leaned forward, resting her forearm against the table.

"I'm eight years older than you."

"I did that math in my head too. I just don't know why it's an issue." Before she could answer, I continued. "I like you and I'd like to get to know you better."

The waitress approached to clear our plates before I could say more. Besides, there are other things we need to discuss, but we don't have to do it all tonight. Hopefully we have the whole summer.

CHAPTER 7

Eve

After the waitress approached to clear our plates, we didn't discuss age again, but I couldn't stop thinking about it. As we left the restaurant and drove home, I fought a mental war while carrying on a normal conversation.

My pole friends seemed to think any age difference is no big deal. And honestly, it shouldn't be. I wouldn't think twice if a man was that much older than a woman he was dating. So why am I so hung up on the reverse?

Max pulled into Aunt Winnie's driveway before I had an answer to that question.

"Would you like to take a walk on the beach before heading inside?"

The weather is perfect and the full moon reflecting off the water looks so beautiful, I'd love to take a closer look.

"I'd like that."

He smiled and stepped out of the truck. I got scolded at

the restaurant when I didn't wait for him to open my door, so I waited for him to do it this time.

I took his hand to steady myself as I stepped down and he held onto it as we made our way across the yard. He let go long enough for me to remove my sandals, but then took it again.

We walked straight toward the water then stopped just shy of the tide. Max directed me in front of him and put his hands on my shoulders. My heart pounded, but I have no idea if it's because of the breathtaking view in front of me or the sexy man behind me.

He stepped closer until his front skimmed my back and rested his chin on my shoulder. His voice vibrated against my ear when he spoke.

"I had a really great time tonight, Eve."

The wind kicked up and I shivered. He slid his hands up and down my arms, warming them before pulling me back against him and wrapping his arms around my waist. I nodded in agreement then leaned my head against his shoulder and enjoyed the view of the moonlight shining off the rippling waves.

"It doesn't matter if you're older than me. How many couples are exactly the same age?" I assumed that was a rhetorical question so I stayed silent. "We're both adults. There's no reason we shouldn't see each other again. Unless you don't want to?"

How could I not? From the first time I laid eyes on Max, I had a feeling of déjà vu. Even now, I feel like I know him, even though we've only spent a few hours together. That has to be a sign of *something*, right? I just need to get over myself, take a chance, and explore whatever it is.

I shook my head, then realized he could interpret that two ways.

Shifting my head slightly to look up at him, I said, "I want to."

The corner of his mouth kicked up into an adorable smile as he turned me in the circle of his arms and pressed his mouth to mine. His kiss was tentative at first, a mere brushing of lips, but it still felt amazing. And that was just the start.

He nibbled at my bottom lip then gently tugged and fully opened his mouth over mine. I dropped my sandals and wrapped my arms around his neck, melting against his chest. I matched his tongue stroke for stroke and our surroundings faded away as all my senses focused on the taste and feel of the man in my arms.

Max tightened his hold, pulling me onto my tiptoes and I groaned as my tight nipples pressed against his hard chest. His mouth was still feasting on mine and with one arm wrapped around my waist holding me in place, he slowly stroked his hand up to cup my breast. Sensation zinged down to my clit when he flicked his thumb against my nipple and I leaned my hips into him, pressing against his erection. He pushed into me once, twice, three times before pulling back slightly to put some space between us. My heels settled onto the sand as Max loosened his hold and slowly ended the kiss.

MAX

I CARRIED THE LAST SHEET OF DRYWALL INTO THE HOUSE AND set it down against the rest of the stack. Pop and I are done building structures at the festival grounds and picked up where we left off on our job list. Today we're hanging drywall in the two-car garage we built for Mitch Beckett last spring. He didn't plan on putting up walls, but his wife didn't like the look of the bare studs. So here we are.

The job should be relatively easy, but it is labor intensive. Which suits me just fine today. It's been two days since my date with Eve and I still get a semi when I think about that kiss. I don't remember the last time I got so turned on while still fully clothed. Probably not since I was a horny teenager. Hopefully the physical work will keep my libido under control.

"We'll start down there," Pop said, pointing to the back wall.

I picked up the drills and set them on the floor over where we'll be working, while he filled his toolbelt with screws. When he was done, he picked up a piece of drywall.

"I can do it," I said.

"So can I."

He walked past me, grumbling under his breath. Instead of arguing with him, I grabbed a sheet, carried it across the garage, and set it next to his. We did that twice more, then started hanging.

"Your mother called last night," he said.

Thankfully he had enough screws in so when I flinched, the drywall didn't fall. He finished securing it to the wall before answering.

"What did she want?"

I set the next sheet into place and waited for him to answer.

"She asked if you're okay." He drilled a screw into place. "Said she's been calling you but you're not picking up and haven't called her back. That true?"

"Yeah."

He shrugged and continued working. I thought he'd say more about their conversation, but as we finished hanging the drywall, he was either quiet or spoke about work.

I looked around the garage, happy with our progress. Aside from a few special cuts, the drywall is hung. When we come back from lunch, one of us will take care of those while the other starts taping the seams.

We normally bring something to eat on site, but we're working right down the block from Whitman's Cafe so decided to eat there instead. It's a win-win as far as I'm concerned. We'll have a delicious lunch and Pop will actually have to take a real break.

The cafe is crowded this time of day, but we found a table for two near the back. After placing our orders, Pop headed to the bathroom to clean up and when he returned, I did the same. As I washed my hands, I chuckled at my reflection. My dark hair is sprinkled with drywall dust, giving it a salt and pepper look. I dampened a paper towel and ran it over my hair to clear out the worst of it then headed back out to the table.

"So why aren't you answering your mother?" Pop asked once I got settled.

"You know she only calls me when she wants something." I took a drink of water then shook my head. "Last time she was badgering me to do that reunion show."

"You should at least answer to see what she wants."

"It will only aggravate me."

I don't know why Pop is essentially sticking up for her. She never calls him either. But I didn't say that. There's no reason to point out what is a touchy subject.

Theoretically I suppose I love my mother, I just don't like her very much. She's the quintessential stage mom and once I removed that element from our relationship, we no longer had one.

"Well, she sounded worried."

I snorted.

"She probably has a deadline for whatever she wants me to sign up for. If she just wanted to reconnect, she'd leave a message stating that."

Our food arrived and the conversation was paused while we dug in. Thinking about my mother always raises my blood pressure, which is why I try to avoid it. Usually it's easy. It's an out of sight, out of mind kind of thing.

I've been living in Seaside working as a handyman for twelve years. I feel so far removed from my life before that, sometimes I can't believe it actually happened. Unfortunately, there's proof of that time showing daily in reruns.

"I'm not getting any younger, you know," Pop said. "I just don't want you to be alone when I'm gone. Your mother is the only family you have."

I popped the last bite of burger into my mouth and chewed as I pondered his words.

"First of all, I don't want to talk or think about a time when you're not here. And second, my mother has let it be known that she only wants one kind of relationship with me and that's not one I'm interested in."

"There has to be a middle ground for the two of you."

"Pop, she wouldn't take my calls for five years after I moved here. *Five years*. And she only called me then because she wanted me to do an interview for one of those stupid where-are-they-now shows." I shook my head. "As if I want people to know where I am now."

"She's getting older too. Maybe she's changed her priorities."

If that was the case, she'd work on her relationship with Pop too, and that hasn't happened.

"I doubt it." I took a drink. "For years I wished Tally Corbin was the kind of mother who made me peanut butter and jelly sandwiches and tucked me in to bed. Instead, she ran me from one audition to another and negotiated contracts."

Our relationship worked until I decided I didn't want to act anymore, which was right around the time I turned eighteen. I was overweight and pre-diabetic, but was reprimanded when I made some lifestyle changes to lose weight. In *Chase and Corbin*, I played the chubby, unpopular geek. The role of handsome ladies' man belonged to my co-star, Chase Collins.

"I didn't think it was all bad. If I did, I would've stepped in."

"It wasn't until I got older and wanted some control," I said. "But I'm grateful for the experience and the fact that Mom always protected me. You know the nightmare lives some child actors had. So it could have been worse."

I'm also grateful for the fact that while my real name is Maxwell Kendrick Corbin, I acted under the name Corbin Kendrick. Obviously that could be discovered with an internet search, but Max Corbin is a common enough name that I haven't had issues with fans knocking on my door. I suppose I have my mother to thank for that, too. Even though I'm not willing to do interviews anymore, she could certainly do them and tell the world what I'm up to these days.

Pop fought me for the bill and he paid, then we walked back to the Beckett garage.

"I'll start taping," he said. "You can fill in the rest of the drywall."

As I got to work, our lunchtime conversation ran through my head. Even though I feel far removed from *Chase and Corbin*, it's very much a part of my life. I haven't mentioned it to the women I spent time with because most of them were transient. Even though we've only had one date, I already know Eve is different. So I suppose I should tell her.

It actually works in my favor that she's a little older than me. She's probably never even seen the show.

CHAPTER 8

Eve

"THIS IS DELICIOUS." AUNT WINNIE SAID BEFORE PLACING another piece of salmon in her mouth.

"Thank you. It's been one of my go-to meals for years. It's fast and the cleanup is easy."

I learned how to make the dish at a cooking class I took years ago. You simply place salmon and zucchini in foil, add seasoning, and toss it on the grill. I usually serve it with jasmine rice, but you can skip the starch if you want to keep it low carb.

"It's been a long time since I had a home-cooked meal."

"Do you ever cook for yourself?"

"Not like this," she said. "Easy things like sandwiches or in the winter I make a pot of chili or soup and have it for a few days."

"I get that. I don't cook a lot since Grace moved away. I usually snack during the day and go out with my pole friends or grab takeout for dinner."

"I'm so happy you started taking those classes."

"Me too. My friend Sophie tried to get me to go for two years." I scooped up a forkful of jasmine rice. "Thankfully I finally gave it a chance."

"It's been good for you."

I nodded as I chewed.

"Both physically and mentally. It's a great workout and learning how to climb the pole and do all the tricks gave me something to focus on besides my divorce."

"Are you going to miss it while you're here?"

"I am, but the break is nice too."

"Have you looked to see if there are any studios close by?"

"No, my plan is to stay active and exercise so I'm not totally out of shape when I get back. But I'm sure there's a studio within a reasonable distance if I wanted to go." I chuckled. "That or I can put up a pole in the house. I'm sure you'd enjoy it too."

A smug smile spread across her face.

"I know a young handyman who could install it for you."

I shook my head and groaned.

"You're way too obvious, Aunt Winnie."

"You never did tell me how your date was Saturday night."

"He took me to a cute Italian bistro and the food was amazing. I had a nice time."

I'm sure she'd love to hear about the fantabulous kiss, but I'm not sharing that. I didn't even tell my pole peeps details, even though they each texted and tried to pry them out of me.

"Any plans for a second date?"

"We're going hiking Wednesday," I said. "I should be home for dinner if you want to go somewhere."

"Don't rush home on my account."

"I won't *rush* home, but we're going sometime in the morning, so I doubt I'll be out too late." I wiped my hands and placed the napkin on my empty plate. "Besides, I'm here to spend time with you."

"You're here to relax and be inspired. I imagine spending time with Max Corbin could be very *inspiring.*" She bobbed her eyebrows. "I won't share anything you do here with your mother or grandmother. What happens at Aunt Winnie's stays at Aunt Winnie's."

"Yeah, I know. I've never been able to find out what my mom did during her summer visits here. But whatever she did, it convinced her to not let me come by myself once I was a teen."

Aunt Winnie laughed then closed her mouth and pretended she locked her lips.

"But seriously, I wish I spent more time here. It's so beautiful." I looked around at the scenery then back at Aunt Winnie. "When my mother wouldn't let me come for extended visits, I swore that once I turned eighteen, I was going to. Then I met John and didn't want to leave him. And you know my mom would have had a stroke if I wanted him to come here with me."

"You can't change the past, so there's no use lamenting about it." She patted my hand. "I believe everything happens for a reason. Who knows what would have happened if you did visit? You could have wanted to stay like I did, or you might have met someone who suited you better than John. Then you wouldn't have Grace."

"You're right."

"I usually am, dear. That's why you should listen to me when I tell you to spend more time with Max. I firmly believe he's the cure to what ails you."

MAX

"IS THIS BORING FOR YOU?" EVE ASKED.

"Nope." She glanced up at me, her brow raised. "It's not."

Even though that's the truth, the trail I originally planned on taking her to today was a little more challenging. Unfortunately, it's closed. Even though she seems to be in decent shape, Eve doesn't have proper hiking boots so I decided to take her somewhere easier. So here we are walking the Soapstone Lake Trail.

Since we got a later start than planned, I suggested having our picnic on the way in. When the trail opened onto the meadow, we stopped and set out the blanket I'd brought and settled onto it, our brown-bag lunches spread out between us. Eve picked up her sandwich and took a bite then looked around as she chewed.

"It's so peaceful here."

"I agree. The other trail I'd planned to take you on had more impressive views, but there's just something about this spot."

"Do you come here often?"

"Generally speaking, I don't hike as much as I used to."

"Why not?"

"My friends and I used to hike all the time, but they're all married now so..." I trailed off and ended the sentence with a shrug. "What about you? Do you hike often?"

"There's a scenic vista near Scranton called Top of the World and my friends and I hike up there once or twice a year."

"What do you do to keep in such great shape?"

Her eyes widened then the corner of her mouth kicked up in a small smile.

"I uh, I do pole dance fitness."

"Pole dance fitness?" She nodded. "Not what I was expecting. How did you start doing that?"

"A friend of mine started taking classes after attending a bachelorette party at the studio. She kept bugging me to go with her, but I insisted I was too busy. Around the time I got divorced, I agreed to take a class. I swear, it was the hardest thing I'd ever done." She smiled. "And I couldn't wait to go back."

Her whole face lit up and I couldn't resist leaning in for a kiss. I don't know why I thought I could stop at a simple peck. Like the other night on the beach, things went from a spark to an explosion as soon as our lips touched.

I nibbled on her luscious bottom lip and she one-upped me by licking at my top lip, fanning the flames. Our mouths opened, our tongues teasing and tasting, giving and taking. I pulled her tight against my chest, savoring every dip and curve of her amazing body.

Eve threaded her fingers through my hair, pulling me closer. She twirled her tongue around mine, drawing it further into her mouth, then lightly sucked. I groaned as my cock jumped, testing the strength of my zipper.

I twisted, lowering Eve to the blanket, our mouths never losing contact. My erection brushed against her hip and I cupped her ass, holding her in place as I pulsed against her. She groaned against my mouth and wrapped her leg around mine, pulling me even closer.

Eve's hands roamed down my back and squeezed my ass before reversing direction and slipping under my shirt.

Goosebumps trailed in the wake of her fingertips as I continued feasting on her mouth.

I don't know how long it went on or what would have happened right there in the meadow if the distinct sound of footsteps didn't break through our sensual fog. I ended the kiss and cocked my head to the side as I listened, my eyes not leaving hers.

The steps moved closer and voices became clear. I squeezed Eve's waist before kneeling and holding out my hand to help her up. She scooted toward the other side of the blanket, her gaze still on mine. When I licked my lips, it dropped to my mouth. I closed my eyes and took a deep breath in through my nose, then let it out slowly. When I opened them again, Eve was watching the people walking a few feet away.

"Ready to start moving again?"

Thankfully she nodded. I don't trust myself to keep my hands off her if we don't. We collected our trash then stood and folded the blanket. I stashed both in my backpack then looped the straps over my shoulders.

More people are on the trail than when we walked in, a few of them with dogs. Eve stopped to say hello to all of them...the dogs, that is.

"Do you have a dog?" I asked when we started walking again.

"No." She shook her head. "I had one growing up, but my ex-husband was allergic."

It's not the first time she mentioned her ex, but the time was never right for me to ask about him. We have about a mile to go before we reach the truck. Now seems like as good a time as any.

"How long has it been since the divorce?"

"Just shy of three years."

"What happened?" I asked, then realized that bordered on being rude. "Sorry, you don't have to answer that."

"No, it's fine," she said. "I found out he started dating a woman at work. From what I understand there were a couple before her, but I didn't know about them. Otherwise, the divorce would have happened sooner."

"That must have been hard."

"It was. When you plan your life a certain way, it's tough to pivot." She shrugged. "Thankfully my daughter is grown and I'm financially independent. It would have been much harder if it happened when she was young, before I started writing."

"How old is your daughter?"

"Grace is twenty-two now, so she was nineteen when it happened." I stopped walking, too shocked to move. "What?" she asked.

It still boggles my mind that she's almost a decade older than me. I shook my head as we started moving again.

"I can't believe you have a daughter that age. You don't look much older than that."

"I started young," she said around a chuckle.

There was more I'd love to ask, but this is a date, not an interrogation. We have plenty of time to get to know each other. Besides, if she tells me hers, eventually she'll expect me to tell her mine and I'm not ready to do that yet. Not all of it anyway.

We approached the truck and I opened the passenger door. Eve climbed in and once she clicked her seatbelt into place, I closed the door. I searched my mind for ideas to extend this date, but only one interests me. As I settled behind the wheel, I prayed it would appeal to her too.

I started the truck and turned down the volume of the radio before turning to face her.

"I'm having a great time and don't want our time together to end just yet," I said. "Would you be interested in coming back to my place? We can sit on the deck and have a drink or two?"

Her eyes searched mine for a few heartbeats.

"I'd like that," she said. Then her mouth curled into a mischievous smile and she added, "Plus, if I go home too early, I'll hear about it from Aunt Winnie."

My answering laugh echoed through the cab as I shifted into drive and pulled out of the parking lot.

CHAPTER 9

Eve

I LOOKED AROUND MAX'S APARTMENT, STILL A LITTLE
shocked that I'm here. The last time I went to a guy's place
after a date, it was a dorm room. So this is all new territory
for me. Although I'll admit that the fluttering in my belly
isn't totally due to nervousness. Anticipation is mixed in too.

My libido has been taking a nap since my divorce. But
since meeting Max, it's not only awake, it's acting like a
hyperactive child.

"I have Summer Shandy, Twisted Tea, or Mike's Hard
Lemonade," Max said from the kitchen area. "Or if you want
non-alcoholic, Sprite or water."

"I'll have a Summer Shandy."

"Would you like a glass?"

"No, the bottle is fine."

He removed the caps, tossed them in the trash, then
joined me on the other side of the counter and handed me
the bottle.

"This is a great space."

"Thanks." He led me toward the French doors on the other side of the living room. "Pop helped me design it. I'm happy with the way it turned out."

I took a drink, then rested my elbows against the railing and took in the view.

"You're right, the view is amazing from up here."

"It was especially amazing the other night when I spotted a certain someone walking toward me on the beach."

Max held his bottle up in a toast then took a drink. My face heated and I flashed a shy smile then looked back out at the ocean.

"I totally understand why Aunt Winnie never came back to Scranton. This place suits her perfectly."

"What about you?"

I shifted to face him.

"What about me?"

"Does it suit you?"

I shrugged.

"I think it's safe to say it suits me perfectly right now. The change of scenery is nice."

He nudged his head toward the Adirondack chairs and we stepped back and took a seat. The view is slightly obscured by the railing, but it's still impressive.

"Have you been able to write?"

"Not yet, but I think I'm getting there."

I explained my newfound plotting process and how I feel the words on the edge of my brain, but can't put them to paper just yet. Or computer, as the case may be. I'm sure he has no idea what I'm talking about...non-writers usually don't...but he listened and actually seemed interested.

"I'm predicting that once you get started, you'll finish this book in record time."

"Say that louder so the universe hears," I said. "But let's not talk about writing anymore. It's boring."

I tipped the bottle to my lips and emptied it. I felt Max watching as I swallowed and shifted my eyes in his direction.

"I don't think anything about you is boring," he said. "In fact, I find you fascinating."

Max's heated stare had me tingling in places that have been dormant for a long time. Imagine what he could do if the rest of his body joined in. The problem is, while the desire is there, I'm in unfamiliar territory here.

I picked at the label on my empty bottle, then looked down at it, as if it's the most fascinating thing in the world.

"Eve?" I glanced over at him. "Are you okay?" I nodded. "I didn't mean to make you uncomfortable."

"You didn't." He raised his brow. "Not really. I'm just–" I gestured as I searched for the best words to explain. "I started dating my ex-husband when I was eighteen and we were married for twenty years. It's been a long time since I dated anyone, much less done anything else."

He placed his bottle on the deck and shifted to better face me.

"Eve."

His voice was low, intimate. The husky sound arousing in its intensity. My gaze met his and I lost myself in his chocolaty depths. Part of me wanted to look away, but I was too mesmerized. He moved closer and continued to speak.

"I really like you and from the moment we met, I felt drawn to you. I'd like to get to know you better, see where this can go." Reaching out, he stroked my cheek, using just his fingertips. "But I hope you know I didn't invite you here expecting anything."

From anyone else, everything he's saying would sound like pathetic lines, but I feel like Max is being honest. It's only fair that I am too.

"I felt that connection too," I said. "And even though I don't think you asked me here because you expected anything to happen, I wouldn't mind if something did. I just might need you to be patient with me."

I put my head down to escape his gaze. Max leaned closer and the arousing combination of his warm skin and sea air drifted to my nose. He took the empty bottle out of my hand and placed it on the deck floor next to his.

"How about if we just take this slow and see where it goes?"

My heart raced and I nodded, not wanting to risk speaking in the breathless voice I was sure would emerge. Placing a gentle hand under my chin, he lifted my mouth to his.

The quick, powerful kiss nearly melted me in my seat and I wanted more. He must have read my mind, because in the next instant, his mouth covered mine again. Summer Shandy lingered on his palate, but as our tongues tangled, I finally got to taste his true essence. The man is delicious.

Max said we should take it slow, but instead I wrapped my hand around the back of his neck and held him close. When that wasn't enough, I threaded my fingers through his hair and curled them into his scalp.

He moved closer, pressing his mouth more fully to mine. I felt him shift and stir, then heard his chair creak. In the next instant, he was on his knees directly in front of me. Easing between my thighs, he wrapped his arms around my lower back, pulling me forward, until our hips and chests touched.

As he continued to feast on my mouth, I felt all his want and need, and gave all mine to him. It's been a long time since I've been kissed, but I don't remember it ever being like this, so raw and consuming. It felt like he was making love to my mouth and I was about to melt into a puddle of desire.

Max broke the kiss, giving us a chance to take a much-needed breath. He looked directly into my eyes, seemingly asking permission to continue. I stroked my hand down the side of his face, enjoying the feel of the stubble that rasped the soft skin of my palm. The corners of my mouth lifted in a small answering smile.

"Are you sure?"

"I've never been more positive of anything in my life."

"Thank fuck."

He leaned forward and tossed me over his shoulder fireman style, then stood and carried me inside as my laughter echoed around us.

MAX

INSTEAD OF DEPOSITING HER ON THE BED, I PLACED EVE gently at its edge. My hands traced every contour and curve of her body before settling on either side of her face. Her blue eyes darkened as she met my gaze.

"You make me crazy, you know that?" I gave her a quick peck and pulled back before it could get out of control.

"Since the day I saw you standing on the porch in that Grumpy nightie, I couldn't stop thinking about you."

She closed her eyes and shook her head.

"That was so embarrassing."

"It was adorable."

I punctuated my words with another kiss. This time, I didn't pull back. We devoured each other, our lips and tongues stroking and savoring, as we gave in to the hunger that we'd kept at bay all day.

Eve wrapped her arms around my neck and I tightened my hold and pulled her closer still, opening my mouth wider, deepening the kiss. Sliding my right hand up her waist, I skimmed the side of her breast, then flicked at her tight nipple with my thumb. Her groan vibrated through my chest and I pulled back just enough to squeeze and mold her to my palm.

Needing to feel her skin on skin, I skimmed my hands down her body then back up, dragging her T-shirt with them. I ended the kiss just long enough to pull it over her head. Her sports bra quickly followed.

I've always been a breast man and hers are pure perfection. I gripped her ass and pulled our hips together as I leaned down and flicked my tongue against her nipple. She let out a low groan and I looked up. Eve's nostrils flared as she watched me take her into my mouth and suck.

Her fingers dug into my scalp and it was my turn to moan when she pressed her hips against the ridge of my erection. I stepped forward, and she stepped back until her thighs rested against the bed. Resting my hands on the small of her back, I eased her down until she was lying on the mattress.

"You are so beautiful."

I traced my fingertips along her stomach, just above the

waistband of her shorts. Popping the button, I slid the zipper down slowly, giving her a chance to stop me if she didn't want this. The material separated, giving me a glimpse of lacy pink panties and I slid my hands into that opening to pull them down. Her hand wrapped around my wrist, halting my movements.

Removing my hands, I straightened and locked my gaze with hers.

"I'm sorry, I–"

"No." She pushed onto her elbows then sat. "I want this. Trust me when I tell you that I *want* this."

Her eyes shifted to the erection that was doing its best to push through my fly. I thought it was going to succeed when she licked her lips as she stared. My low groan broke the spell and she met my gaze again.

"I just think I'd be more comfortable if I wasn't the only one not wearing clothes."

Keeping my gaze locked to hers, I whipped my shirt over my head and tossed it to the floor. Unbuttoning my shorts, I started to lower them but she stopped me again.

Eve sat and shifted forward, and with her eyes locked on mine, tucked her hands into my open waistband. Sliding them around to my back, she cupped my ass beneath my boxer briefs. After giving it a squeeze, she dragged them down until they pooled around my ankles.

My cock bobbed right in front of her face. She nibbled at her bottom lip for what seemed like forever before reaching out and wrapping her hand around it. I took in a deep breath through my nose and let it out slowly through my mouth. It's been a while and her touch is the sweetest form of torture.

She stroked and explored, seeming fascinated. I closed my eyes and groaned as her hand moved up and down, then settled into a slow, sensual rhythm. It was my turn to wrap my hand around her wrist to halt her movements.

"That feels *really* good," I said with an awkward chuckle. "*Too good.*"

"Isn't it supposed to feel good?"

Goosebumps covered my entire body when she dragged her fingers along my shaft then squeezed the head before letting go.

"Not yet." Wrapping my hands around her waist, I shifted her back to the middle of the bed and followed her down. "Not until you feel *good* at least once."

I leaned down and kissed Eve's stomach, nipping at her navel before continuing upward to lick at first one nipple then the other. Setting my mouth on her right breast, our eyes held as I ran my tongue around it, slowly spiraling toward her nipple. As I sucked, Eve's back arched and she let out a long, low groan.

"Max."

My name came out more as a sigh than a word

I moved onto her left breast, offering it the same treatment.

"Hmm?"

When she didn't answer, I continued what I was doing until her hips thrust against me. Goosebumps trailed in my wake as I ran my fingers over her stomach. Her hips pressed up, shifting my fingertips onto the waistband of her panties.

"Please."

I released her nipple and nibbled my way across her chest, over her collarbone, and up her neck.

"Please what?" I whispered against her ear.

"Touch me. Please touch me."

She sounded almost desperate. If what she said is true

and she hasn't been with anyone since her divorce, I can understand why.

Shifting onto my knees, I hooked my fingers into her waistband and backed away just enough to pull her panties and shorts off in one swipe. Eve watched as I leaned forward and kissed her knee before nibbling my way up. When I settled between her thighs and placed an open-mouthed kiss at their juncture, she nearly jumped off the bed. I laid a restraining hand on her belly and met her gaze over the expanse of her body.

With our eyes locked on each other, I licked through her folds then flicked the tiny nub of nerves with the tip of my tongue. She closed her eyes and let out a long, low moan and tangled her fingers into my hair.

I slipped my middle finger through her slick folds and began a steady in-and-out motion as my tongue circled her clit.

"Max, that feels so good."

Good isn't nearly good enough. I added my index finger and increased the rhythm then shifted back and circled her clit with my thumb. Eve's breath came out in shallow pants and I knew she was close. Time to push her over the edge.

I trailed kisses up her stomach to her breasts and alternately sucked one nipple then the other in time with the ministrations of my hands.

She dug her fingers into my shoulders and arched her back.

"Max, I'm gonna–"

Her words ended on a low, guttural moan.

CHAPTER 10

Eve

"Wow." I barely recognized my voice. "That was amazing."

"Amazing is better than good, right?"

"I believe it is."

The corner of Max's mouth curled up at my words, but his smile looked strained. And I totally get it. Even after that amazing orgasm, I'm still a little on edge.

Shifting back, I rested against the pillows and held out my arms. Max's cock bobbed against his stomach as he crawled toward me. Before he reached me, his eyes widened and he shifted then reached over to retrieve a foil packet from the drawer of the bedside table. I watched as he ripped it open and rolled the condom down his impressive length.

My heartbeat had just returned to normal, but it pounded again when Max settled between my thighs. I haven't been in this position with anyone besides my ex-husband so it should feel strange or awkward, but that's not the case. It feels oh so right.

He locked his gaze to mine then pressed forward. It's been a *long* time for me and at first my body resisted the intrusion, but he was patient and inch by slow inch, he slipped inside. Closing my eyes, I let out a breath once we were completely joined.

Max kissed my forehead, the tip of my nose, and my mouth.

"You doing okay?"

I opened my eyes and met his concerned gaze.

"I'm wonderful."

He kissed me again then slowly pulled out then pushed back in. Then did it again and again, picking up the pace each time, until he settled into a steady rhythm designed to make me lose my mind. Pressing my feet against the mattress, I pushed my hips up, meeting his every thrust.

"Eve, you feel so amazing."

His hands cupped my ass and tilted my hips. Wanting to feel more, *needing* to feel more, I wrapped my legs around his waist and he sank even deeper. Max picked up the pace and I got sucked into the sensation. I didn't think it could get any better, but he proved me wrong.

"Hold on."

I barely processed those two words when he tightened his grip on my ass and rolled, putting his back against the bed with me on top, straddling his hips. I thought he'd been deep before, but this position made me sink down until he filled me completely.

Resting my hands against his chest, I rose up on my knees then moved back down. I did that until my thighs threatened to cramp then settled into a forward and back motion. Max reached up and cupped my breasts, flicking his thumbs over my nipples again and again, sending a zing of sensation right to my clit. My inner muscles clenched and tightened around him and I picked up the pace.

"*Max.*"

He sat and wrapped his hands around my hips, helping me keep a steady rhythm as his mouth opened over my breast. Moving back and forth, he nipped, licked, and sucked. Pleasure radiated between my nipples and my pussy and I moved faster and faster, then shifted my hips to grind my clit against him.

That did it.

I let out a long, hoarse moan as I came for the second time. Max thrust up into me and let out his own shout before resting back against the pillows and pulling me on top of him. I rested my head against his chest and closed my eyes.

MAX

EVE'S WARM BREATH FLOATED OVER MY CHEST AND I LOVED the feel of her snuggled on top of me. Unfortunately, I need to move and take care of business before things get messy.

"Eve."

"Hmm?"

I stroked my hands down her back and kissed the top of her head.

"I need to move."

"Oh my God, I'm sorry." She jerked up and shifted to slide off me. "I'm probably crushing you."

"You're not crushing me." I held her in place and waited

until she looked me in the eye. "I need to go to the bathroom to take care of the condom."

Her cheeks turned pink and this time when she moved, I let her.

I slipped out of bed, walked across the room to the bathroom, and closed the door behind me. The after of sex can be a little awkward, especially the first time. Eve was with the same person forever, so I imagine this is even more strange for her.

I'm sure her mind is running a mile a minute right now, so I don't want to leave her alone too long. I took care of business as quickly as possible, washed my hands, and headed back to bed.

Eve sat against the pillows, her hands holding the blanket in place beneath her chin. She had a slight deer-in-the-headlights look as her gaze met mine.

"Hey." I slipped into bed next to her. "What's wrong?"

I shifted under the covers and pulled her into my arms. She rested her head against my chest, but still felt stiff.

"I wasn't sure what to do. Getting dressed to leave while you were in the bathroom seemed kind of strange, so I got under the covers. But just sitting here, naked, in your bed seemed weird too."

I kissed the top of her head.

"I like having you naked in my bed." Just like I'd hoped, she chuckled at my words and relaxed a little. "But seriously, I'm glad you didn't get dressed to leave."

"I just don't want to do anything inappropriate."

"Like what?"

"I don't know." She shrugged. "I don't even know what's appropriate now and what's not. It's been more than two decades since I did this. Things were a lot different then."

"Why don't you just do what feels natural and we'll take it from there?"

Eve nodded then wrapped her arm around my waist, relaxing a little more. I took that as a good sign. Eventually her breathing slowed and settled into a steady rhythm.

I closed my eyes, unable to wipe the sappy smile from my face. Being with Eve is just...easy. And for the first time in a long time, I want more than just a casual hookup. Hopefully she feels the same. But we can discuss that later, after our nap.

CHAPTER 11

Eve

Max turned into the driveway and I was grateful when I didn't see Gertrude in her usual spot. That means Aunt Winnie isn't home. There's no doubt in my mind she'd take one look at me and know what Max and I have been up to for the past several hours. Granted, I'm a grown woman and have nothing to feel guilty about, but I'd still feel awkward. Once I process everything, I'll have a better game face.

"Thank you for today," he said.

"Thank *you*. I had an amazing time."

"Enough that you'd want to repeat it?"

I couldn't stop the slow smile that spread across my face. "Definitely."

"Tomorrow night?"

"So soon?"

"You're lucky I have to work in the morning or I'd be picking you up for breakfast."

He leaned closer and pressed his lips to mine. Like most

other times we kissed, it didn't stop at a quick peck. Sliding his right hand across my jaw, Max wrapped his long fingers into my hair and tilted my head back and to the side. His mouth opened over mine, taking the kiss to a whole other level. I held onto his biceps as our tongues tangled together.

Max shifted his hands down my back and wrapped them around my waist. He pulled me over the console until I rested against his chest. I was a heartbeat away from inviting him inside when Max changed the tempo of the kiss from hot and hungry to sweet and soothing. He kissed each corner of my mouth then rested his forehead against mine.

"I should let you get inside."

He loosened his hold on my waist, and I slid back into my seat. I nodded and watched as he stepped out of the truck. My fingers tingled when I placed my hand in his as he helped me down and walked me to the door.

"I'll pick you up at six tomorrow night?"

"Perfect."

Leaning forward, he kissed me on the cheek and stepped back while I opened the door. He nodded then turned and walked back to the truck. I watched as he slipped behind the steering wheel and waved before closing the door.

I filled a tumbler with ice and added water then headed up to my room. After setting the drink on my desk, I walked into the bathroom, plugged the tub, and turned on the water. After hiking, not to mention all my other activities, a good soak will feel good.

Digging through the welcome basket Aunt Winnie made me, I found Epsom salts and tossed two handfuls into the water. Just for good measure, I added a few drops of lavender essential oil. Soon a scented steam filled the room. I stripped then stepped into the water, taking time to adjust to the heat. My low moan echoed through the room as I rested my head against the edge of the tub.

I closed my eyes and thought about the day. When Max invited me out for a hike, I never expected to end up at his place having sex...three times. Well technically two and a half, I guess. I'd shocked myself with that. Oral sex has never been high on my list of things to do, but it seems that's changed. It seems a lot has changed.

My mouth curled into a smile at that last thought. After years of no sex, what I'd expected to be awkward was an amazing experience. I have Max to thank for that.

He mentioned more than once that he wants to get to know me better and see where this can go. I'm all for the former but not sure about the latter. After all, I have a life on the other side of the country. But I'm not going to obsess about that right now. I'll just enjoy spending time with Max and take things as they come.

I flexed my pruney fingers and decided it was time to get out. After pulling out the stopper with my toes, I stood, then stepped out of the tub and wrapped myself in a fluffy robe.

I studied my reflection in the mirror as I towel-dried my hair. I'm sure my rosy glow isn't only from the hot bath. There's nothing like great sex to add color to your cheeks.

Rummaging through the welcome basket again, I found the bottle of lotion and slathered it all over my damp skin. Once that soaked in, I shrugged into a comfy T-shirt and joggers.

I walked across the room and settled into the chair behind the desk. Opening my laptop, I clicked on the file I'd started for my new book. The notebook where I'd "semi-plotted" sat open next to my right hand. I looked down at it and deciphered my handwriting then set my fingers on the home keys and started to type.

Max

I FINISHED MIXING THE CONCRETE AND SET THE HOE DOWN IN the wheelbarrow. I've wanted to get a cement mixer for years, but Pop likes to do things the old-fashioned way. I tend to pick my battles and that one didn't make the list. Besides, it's a good workout.

"You done over there?"

"Yep."

I tipped the wheelbarrow forward and rolled it over next to where he'd just finished putting in forms. Grabbing the shovel, I filled them with concrete until the bucket was empty. While I mixed a fresh batch, Pop pulled the screen board across the forms with a back-and-forth sawing motion, evening out the concrete, and removing the excess. Then he picked up the flattening tool and smoothed the surface while I poured the next batch.

We repeated that process until fresh sidewalks lined the front and side of the house.

I hosed out the wheelbarrow while he finished up.

"What kind of sandwiches do we have?" he asked when he was done.

"Ham or roast beef."

I took his tools and cleaned them off then handed him the hose and picked up a towel to dry my hands.

We have about thirty minutes until the excess water is forced to the surface of the concrete and Pop can joint and edge it. I pulled two folding chairs out of the bed of my truck and set them up. He took a seat as I rummaged in the cooler. I held up one of each sandwich.

"Roast beef."

I handed him the sandwich and a bottle of water then sat and dug into my own.

"You've been spending a lot of time with Winnie's niece."

"Yeah," I said, then took a big bite.

"Guess you like her."

I nodded as I chewed and swallowed, then took a drink. I'm not sure what this conversation is about. In all the years I've lived here, Pop has never commented on who I "spend time with." Other than stating he thinks there've been too many, that is.

It must be because of whatever the thing is between him and Winnie. He probably thinks he'll be in hot water with her if I do something to screw up with Eve. I decided to set his mind at ease.

"I like Eve. She's really great and fun to hang around with."

He grunted and finished his sandwich.

"Does she know?"

I stopped mid-chew.

"About what?"

"Does she know about the show?" Pop looked at me like I had the brain of a gnat and shook his head. "What else would I be talking about?"

"No."

I finished my water and crumbled the bottle.

"Don't you think you should tell her?"

"I will," I said. "I'm just waiting for the right time."

"When's that gonna be?"

"I don't know. Like I said, I haven't found it yet."

He grunted.

"Just don't wait too long."

I thought about that for a minute then asked the question that's been swirling in my head for the past couple weeks.

"Do you think it's really that big of a deal?"

Pop stood and stretched then walked over to check the concrete. I didn't think he was going to answer, but then he turned and shrugged.

"I don't know. Only she can tell you that."

He walked over to the tools and picked up his edger. I stood and watched as he moved the tool back and forth, using the form as a guide to create perfect edges. He makes it look easy, but I know for a fact it's not. I can do it if necessary, but it takes me twice as long and doesn't turn out as nice as when he does it.

I followed Pop as he moved down the sidewalks doing his thing.

"I'm not hiding anything from Eve," I said, picking up our conversation. "I just...that part of my life is behind me. It doesn't even seem like that was me."

"But it *was* you." He sat back on his heels and looked up at me. "And maybe I'm old-fashioned, but I think that when you're getting to know someone, you want to know all about them, not just bits and pieces."

Pop is a man of few words, but the ones he speaks are usually right on point.

"You're right." I dragged my fingers through my hair and let out a deep breath. "I'll find the right time."

CHAPTER 12

Eve

"So, it's been a few weeks now. How are things going with *Max*?"

Anjannette dragged out the name, turning the single syllable into three.

"Things are great. We're having a good time."

"And the book?" Keera asked.

"I'm happy to say the words have been flowing. I just passed the halfway point this morning."

Keera screeched and clapped her hands.

"I told you getting the juices flowing would help," Sophie said.

I rolled my eyes.

"Well, I guess I can't argue with you since I literally started this book the night after Max and I had sex for the first time."

"So what have you guys been doing? Besides boning." Keera asked.

"Boning?" I snort-laughed. "I haven't heard that word since high school."

"It's retro." She shrugged. "And just answer the question."

"We've just been doing regular date stuff. You know, dinner, hiking, walks on the beach. Tomorrow night we're having dinner and watching a movie at his place."

"Ooh, a Netflix and chill night," Anjannette said.

"I've used that term in my books, but didn't even realize that's what we'd be doing. Now I'm even more excited about the date. I'll be checking an item off my bucket list I didn't even know was on there."

"You know, as much as I miss you, I'm so happy you went to Seaside. Even through my crappy computer, I can see how good it's been for you. You're totally glowing," Keera said. "And I swear it has nothing to do with the fact that you're writing again."

She drew a cross over her heart with her fingers as she said that last sentence.

"What does Aunt Winnie think about you and Max canoodling?" Sophie asked.

"In true Aunt Winnie fashion, she thinks it's wonderful. I told you, she was lobbying for us to get together from the start."

"What about Grace?" Anjannette asked.

"I haven't told her."

"Are you going to?"

"Probably not." I scrunched my nose. "I don't think I need to, do you?" Before they could answer, I continued. "I mean, I'll be back in Scranton at the end of the summer so it's not like this can go anywhere."

Even though that thought has been in the back of my

mind since Max and I got involved, somehow saying it out loud makes it more real. And more depressing.

"You never know. Things always work out in our novels. Maybe real life will mimic our art," Sophie said.

"You might want to at least casually mention Max to Grace just in case he ends up being her step-daddy." Keera bobbed her eyebrows.

I rolled my eyes.

"Now you're getting way ahead of yourself," I said. "Besides, Grace isn't telling me about the boys she's dating out in England."

"How do you know she's dating anyone?"

"Because she's an accent whore just like her mama. Those guys would be hard to resist."

I stuck my tongue out to punctuate my words then took a sip of wine. Anjannette opened her mouth to say something but I waved my hand in front of my camera to halt her words.

"Enough about me. Tell me what's going on at the studio."

Eventually I'll have to figure out how Max and I are going to handle the end of the summer, but I'll put that off for as long as I can.

MAX

"SORRY ABOUT THE TAKEOUT. I'D PLANNED ON COOKING, BUT ended up working later than expected."

I had just enough time to pick up the food, get home, and take a quick shower before Eve arrived.

"No, this is great."

We spread the assortment of appetizers I'd brought home from Mo's Seafood and Chowder out on the coffee table.

"Rough day?" she asked as she filled her plate.

"No, the opposite actually," I said as I did the same. "Pop planned on the job taking two days, but by three o'clock, we were eighty percent finished, so we decided to push and finish today." I smiled. "That means I have tomorrow off."

"That's a nice surprise."

"It definitely is." I popped a piece of shrimp into my mouth and settled against the arm of the couch. "How'd the writing go today?"

"Wonderful. I finished the black moment right before I headed over here."

Before meeting Eve, I wouldn't have had a clue what that means. But now I know it's the point in the book where the happily-ever-after is in peril. I also know that it means she's at least three-quarters done writing the book.

"That's awesome."

"I'm so happy the words are flowing again. When I couldn't write, I was so scared my career was over." She chuckled. "I wouldn't know how to act if I had to go out and get a *real* job."

"From what you've told me about writing and marketing books, your job is as real as it gets."

"You know what they say, 'Love what you do and you won't work a day in your life.'"

"Truer words have never been spoken."

"Do you love being a handyman?"

I thought about how to answer that as I finished chewing a crab Rangoon.

"Love is a strong word. I mean, I enjoy the work. But what I like most about it is working with Pop."

"That's really sweet."

"He seems like a curmudgeonly old coot sometimes, but he invited me to move in with him when I had nowhere to go and no plan. Then he hired me as his assistant and had the patience of a saint as he taught me the necessary skills."

"So you didn't take classes or anything?"

"Nope, Pop taught me everything I know."

I finished the last bite on my plate and set it on the coffee table. Before Eve asked more about my education or work background, I decided to change the subject.

"Did you have a movie in mind?"

Picking up the remote, I turned on the TV and pulled up the apps.

"I don't," she said. "I've never had a Netflix and chill night so I'm not sure which genre is best."

I raised my brow.

"Is that what this is?"

"When I told my pole ladies what we were doing tonight, they labeled it as such."

"If the pole ladies said it, it must be true." I clicked on Netflix. "Let me know if something catches your eye."

"Besides you?"

She flashed a sexy smirk that turned into a giggle. Placing the remote on the coffee table, I moved over to sit next to her.

"We could chill and Netflix."

I tugged at her shirt to expose her collarbone then I kissed my way across it and up her neck.

"Mmm, that sounds like a wonderful idea."

CHAPTER 13

Eve

Max nibbled my earlobe then dragged his mouth along my cheek and pulled back just far enough to look me in the eye.

"You think so?"

"I definitely do."

Placing his hands on either side of my waist, Max pulled me down until my head rested against the arm of the couch. He settled into the apex of my thighs and opened his mouth over mine. I looped my arms around his neck and met him stroke for stroke. He deepened the kiss, thrusting his hips in time with our tangling tongues, pressing his erection against my heat.

I slipped my hands into the waistband of his shorts and squeezed his ass, encouraging him to thrust harder. Max eagerly complied and I couldn't hold back little whimpers each time he pushed against me.

He pressed my hip against the couch, stopping me from moving and slowly ended the kiss.

"You drive me crazy, you know that?"

I stared back at him with dazed eyes.

"Really?"

"My cock is ready to explode right now." He pushed against me. "I'm thirty-three years old and after some heavy petting on the sofa, I'm ready to come in my shorts."

I bit my bottom lip as my mouth curled into a satisfied smile. It always both surprises and pleases me when he tells me things like that. I still can't believe he finds me *that* attractive, that *sexy* as he always says.

He sat back and just looked at me for several heartbeats. Too many.

"What?" I asked.

"I was just thinking that with your swollen lips, flush cheeks, and tousled hair, you look like a wet dream come true."

"Max."

His name came out as a soft sigh. I had started to cool off, but his words made me throb with want again. He lowered his head and kissed his way across my cheek to my ear.

"I thought about picking you up and carrying you to the bedroom, but another idea crossed my mind."

"What's that?"

"How about if I just show you?"

Shifting to stand, he took my hand and pulled me up. I watched as he whipped off his shirt then lowered his shorts. His erection peeked over the waistband of his boxer briefs and I fought the urge to reach out and touch it. But he seems to have a plan here. Who am I to interfere with that?

He removed my shirt and bra, then slipped his fingers

into the elastic waistband of my shorts and pushed. They dropped down my legs and pooled at my ankles. I stepped out of them, eager to find out what he has planned.

"Turn around."

I did as he told me and he stepped closer, pressing his erection against the curve of my back before moving back just far enough to pull my underwear down. When he stood behind me again, his naked cock bobbed against me.

"Look at the French doors."

I lifted my gaze and looked across the room. Dusk had fallen and the fiery orange sky is absolutely gorgeous.

"It's beautiful," I said.

He shifted my hair to the side and pressed closer to kiss my neck. Moisture pooled between my thighs at the feel of him against me. As if he sensed that, Max moved his hand down my arm and over my hip. His fingers skimmed against my folds before he slipped his middle finger between them to circle my clit. His other hand cupped my breast and plucked my distended nipple between his thumb and forefinger.

The two sensations mingled together deep in my belly and shot to every erogenous zone in my body. I stiffened my legs and pressed my back against his chest to avoid crumbling to the floor.

"Focus on the glass instead of the view."

His warm breath against my ear added to the sensation and I let out a low groan.

It took my sex-addled brain a second to figure out what he wanted me to do, but finally I shifted my gaze and spotted our reflection in the glass.

"Do you see us?" I nodded. "Good. Keep your eyes focused right there. I want you to watch me make you come."

My entire body broke out in goosebumps at his words. I've never done anything like this in my life. But I'll admit, it's hot as hell.

The glass didn't offer a clear reflection, but as Max teased and touched me, my mind filled in the blanks and I saw everything like it was in technicolor.

He slipped his finger inside me before pulling back to circle my clit, then did it again. And again. And again. As if that wasn't enough, his other fingers alternately squeezed and twisted my nipple. Urging me to lean back against him, he slid his hand across my chest and gave my other nipple the same treatment.

"Oh God Max, I'm–" I lost my breath as he circled and pressed my clit before slipping through my folds to finger fuck me again. "I'm gonna come."

"Are you watching?"

"Yes."

My voice sounded as desperate as I felt.

He lowered his mouth to my ear and nibbled at the lobe before licking at the whorl. The sensory overload continued as he flicked his thumb over one nipple then the other while pressing against then pinching my clit.

It was all too much.

The tingles started in my nipples then radiated down to my pussy. Max slipped his fingers inside me and my inner walls contracted around them as the palm of his hand pressed against my mound.

He slowly slid his fingers out and nudged me toward the couch.

"Rest your knee on the arm." My legs felt like jelly but I managed to do it. "Now move your other leg over as far as you can."

I heard him rip open a foil packet and a second later, he

wrapped his arm around my waist and urged me to bend forward just a little bit.

"Keep watching."

It had gotten darker outside so our reflection was a little sharper. I watched as he bent his knees and dipped slightly behind me, then I felt his cock press against my entrance and slowly slip inside until he completely filled me.

"Mmm, you're so tight. It feels so fucking good," he said against my neck.

He moved in and out, settling into a rhythm designed to drive me crazy. My inner walls gripped him each time he retreated and welcomed him back with every forward thrust. Thankfully he kept his arm wrapped around my waist because I probably would have crumbled to the floor when he circled my clit, setting off my second orgasm in less than five minutes.

Max

I spooned Eve from behind, enjoying the feel of her against me. Her breathing was deep and even so I was surprised when she spoke.

"I've never done anything like that."

"Did you like it?"

Her hair brushed against my chin as she nodded.

"I did."

I've had mirror sex before, but haven't done anything like what we just did. She doesn't need to know that first part though.

"When I first moved in here, sometimes my reflection in

the glass would scare me. Then one night, I was sitting on the couch and the idea of what we just did popped into my head. I was just waiting for the right person to do it with."

She turned her head to look back at me.

"Was it worth the wait?"

"Oh yeah." She turned back around and I pulled her closer. "We never did Netflix after chilling. Do you want to watch something now?"

"Sure."

I turned and reached over to grab the remote off the nightstand behind me and clicked on the TV.

"What kind of movies do you like?"

Eve rolled over to face me as the Netflix menu filled the screen.

"I'll watch pretty much anything besides scary movies." She scrunched her nose. "I don't like a lot of blood and gore either."

I scrolled down to the comedies and one caught my eye.

"How about *Just Go With It*?"

"Ooh, I love Adam Sandler movies."

After pressing play, I wrapped my arm around Eve's shoulders and invited her to rest her head against my chest. She rested her arm against my waist and settled in.

As the movie started, I tried to remember if I've ever been this intimate with a woman. I mean, I've had sex with plenty of women, probably too many, but this relaxed closeness is rare for me.

The only thing I came up with is my girlfriend when I was eighteen. She was the first girl I had sex with, and I thought I was in love. All these years later, I still don't know if I was or not. Either way, it didn't matter because she was only using me, hoping my mother would represent her.

I'm not sure what it says about me that it's been so many

years since I've formed any sort of real bond with a woman says about me. What I do know is that this thing with Eve is all-consuming. I have so many thoughts, feelings, and emotions swirling through me, sometimes it's hard to process everything. Since the moment I met Eve, I was hooked. And the more time we spend together, the deeper it goes.

I shifted my attention back to the movie just in time to see Jennifer Aniston strut into the restaurant after having a makeover.

"She is absolutely gorgeous," Eve said. "She was my age when she made this movie and look at her. Flawless."

"You're pretty flawless yourself."

"Why thank you sir." Her exaggerated Southern accent made me chuckle. She kissed my chest and curled her fingers into my waist. "You're pretty perfect too."

I don't know about that, but we are perfect together. In my opinion anyway. Things with Eve are just...*easy*. We get along well, the sex is incredible, and whenever I'm not with her, it's like part of me is missing. I haven't put a name to what I'm feeling yet, but I've watched my friends fall in love one-by-one so I know the signs.

Eve is scheduled to leave in five weeks. I need to tell her how I feel sooner rather than later. If I get lucky she'll extend her visit with Winnie. Otherwise, I'd be open to figuring out how to make a cross-country relationship work.

But before that, there's another conversation that needs to happen.

Pop seems to think my past is a big deal, but I'm hoping it won't matter. We got over the whole age thing and, in my opinion, that's a bigger issue than what I did for a living before I moved to Seaside. So I'm hopeful, even though I keep putting off having the conversation. But I know we have to have it soon.

CHAPTER 14

Eve

MAX AND I WALKED THROUGH THE FARMER'S MARKET HAND-in-hand. The weather is perfect for spending time outside, which is good because we're here now then heading to the music festival for the rest of the day.

"This is bigger than I thought it'd be," I said.

"It's definitely grown over the years." He gestured to the right. "Winnie's down that way."

I turned and we followed the makeshift road, stopping at various vendors along the way. The temptation to buy all the things was strong, but I restrained myself. I don't want to have to lug tons of stuff on the plane. I've been collecting business cards along the way from people who have online stores so I can order once I get home.

"I may buy some things and just ship them before I leave." I shrugged. "It's nice hand-picking items instead of ordering from a website."

We approached a booth of organic lotions. I picked up a bottle that I recognized.

"Aunt Winnie made me a welcome basket and this was in it. It smells amazing."

I popped open the top and sniffed then held it out for Max to do the same.

"Mmm, that smells like you." His smile was pure sin. "And I agree, it's amazing."

Since I've been slathering myself with it after every shower, it makes sense that he'd recognize the scent.

"I'm going to grab this, I'm almost out."

"It's on me." Max took the bottle out of my hand. "After all, it brings me so much pleasure."

He leaned down and brushed his mouth against mine before stepping over to pay.

"Excuse me." I turned toward the voice. "Aren't you Everly Reese?"

"Yes." I'd raised my voice at the end of the word, turning it into a question, so I added more confidently, "Yes I am."

"Oh my God! I can't believe I'm meeting you." She shook my hand and held on as she continued. "You're my favorite author. I've read every single one of your books, some multiple times. I *can't wait* for the new release in a couple weeks."

She finally paused for a breath so I took the opportunity to jump in.

"I'm so glad you enjoy my books. What's your name?"

"Mona." She'd never released my hand and started shaking it again. "Mona Potter."

"It's nice to meet you."

"Oh my God. I still can't believe this."

I felt Max return to my side and introduced him. He

must have overheard our conversation, because as he shook her hand, he said, "So you're a big fan of Everly's?"

"I am," she said. "Anytime I see a book signing, I always check to see if you'll be there in hopes that I could meet you."

"I'm sorry. I haven't done signings in a few years."

At the beginning of my career, I did some signings, mostly connected to writers' conferences I attended. Now I do signed paperback sales a couple times a year instead.

We chatted for a few more minutes, mostly about my books and Mona's love of them. But she also mentioned how happy she is to see I've moved on from my divorce with a "nice, hot boyfriend."

"Email me your information and I'll send you an ARC of the new book."

She screeched, drawing the attention of several people walking by. They continued moving when they realized nothing bad was happening.

"I can't believe I'll have the book early. Thank you so much!"

"You're very welcome," I said.

Max took a picture of Mona and me both on her phone and mine, and we continued on our way to Aunt Winnie's booth.

"I feel like I'm with a celebrity."

"I'm in shock," I said. "I've never been recognized in public before."

If I was surprised to be recognized, I was even more so when I saw Henry Corbin in Aunt Winnie's booth. Not *by* it, just visiting. *In* it, wrapping a painting in brown paper.

"Are Aunt Winnie and your grandfather *together*?"

"That's a complicated question, but the simple answer is no."

Before he could expand on that, we approached the booth and joined the crowd that surrounded it. Aunt Winnie may be *hippy-dippy* but she's also a shrewd businesswoman and when people find out she's selling her paintings in person somewhere, they come out in droves.

She saw Max and me and excused herself from the people she was speaking with.

"I figured we'd stop by, say hi, and confirm dinner plans," I said. "We had a couple ideas but didn't really decide what we're doing."

"Henry is joining us so how about if we just meet you at The Rusty Skipper at six? Does that give you enough time at the music festival?"

She directed that question at Max. Which makes sense because I honestly have no idea.

"More than enough," he said.

More people approached the table, a few of them pointed at Winnie.

"We'll let you get back to your adoring fans," I said. "See you at six."

She gave both Max and me a kiss on the cheek and we both said goodbye to Henry before heading toward the exit. On the way out, I slowed and looked at every booth, fighting the urge to stop.

"You can stop if you want," Max said.

"No, that's fine. We've already been here longer than planned. I'll come back before I leave to buy some things."

He looked like he was going to say something but stopped when someone called his name.

MAX

. . .

I looked over to see Dex and Courtney approaching with the twins. Thank God. Eve has mentioned going back to Scranton multiple times today. Talking to them will be a nice distraction to keep me from saying something stupid like, "Maybe you should stay longer."

Eventually I will say that, but like Pop always says, "There's a time and a place for everything." On the way out of the farmer's market is neither of those.

I introduced Eve to Dex and Courtney.

"And those sleepy guys are Andrew and Aaron," I said.

"They're so adorable," she said.

"We come here every week and plan the outing for nap time," Courtney said.

"That's smart."

"Thankfully once they're out, they'll sleep through anything." She smiled at her husband. "Just like their father."

"I should act insulted, but I can't," Dex said. "She's right. I can sleep anywhere and through anything. All in all, it's a good trait to pass on to kids, right?"

"From a mother of a former colicky child who didn't sleep for almost a year, I say it's a great trait to pass on," Eve said.

I listened to them talk about sleep schedules and other baby-related things for a few minutes before Dex totally changed the subject.

"I was actually going to call you," he said. "Do you have a roofing nail gun I can borrow for a day? I'm helping Courtney's dad replace the roof on his garage and if you remember, the last time I did something like that with a hammer, my hand was curled into a fist for a week."

"That's his story and he's sticking to it," I said to Courtney.

"You're an ass," Dex said, even though he was laughing.

"Maybe, but I'm an ass with an extra roofing nail gun. In fact, it's in my truck." I looked at Eve. "Do you mind hanging out here with Courtney and the boys while we go grab it?"

"No, not at all," she said.

I gave her a quick kiss and Dex and I headed to my truck.

"So that's Eve."

"That's Eve."

"She seems nice. Things are still going well?"

I hesitated for a second before saying, "Yeah."

"That didn't sound very confident."

As we approached the truck, I used every second before retrieving the nail gun to figure out what to say to that.

"I really like her, Dex."

"So what's the problem?"

I looked down at the ground and rubbed the back of my neck.

"For one thing, she's leaving in a month."

"And for another?"

"I haven't told her about my past yet."

"Do you think it will matter?"

"I don't see why it would." I shrugged. "But Pop seems to think it will."

The fact that I was a child star is kind of a well-known secret in Seaside, especially with the older folks. It was more of a thing when I first moved here, but after twelve years, no one really cares or talks about it.

"What do you think?" I asked.

"Could go either way."

I handed Dex the nail gun and we headed over to the next aisle to put it in his truck.

"I'm gonna ask her to extend her trip."

His eyes rounded.

"Do you think she will?"

I've been thinking about that for the past week and still don't know the answer.

"No idea."

He patted me on the shoulder as we walked back to the entrance of the farmer's market. The sight of Eve made me smile.

"I'm sorry you're in turmoil here, but you have to understand how enjoyable it is for me to watch. The guys and I have been wondering when you'd fall. And that sappy smile leaves no doubt that you've fallen hard."

"I'm not denying it."

"Then you just have to put yourself out there and hope for the best."

Eve and I are going to enjoy the music festival today, and then tomorrow we'll have a serious talk.

CHAPTER 15

Eve

My alarm chimed and I reached over to turn it off. I glanced at the clock wondering where the day went. I'm meeting Max on the beach and we're walking down to his place for dinner. But first, Grace should be calling.

That last thought just crossed my mind when my computer, phone, and iPad buzzed at the same time. I opened the app on my computer and Grace's face appeared on my screen.

"Hi honey!"

"Mom! I just found out that I aced my third paper!" she said.

"That's amazing! Congratulations!"

She'd been texting grades from papers and tests through the week, but was waiting on this last one to come in. After telling me the grade she received, and explaining its equivalent to US grades and filled me in on her week. Lots of classes and studying, but also fun times with friends. Most parents would be worried about the former, but I'm just as concerned about the latter. But I'm fortunate because Grace has always been a good student.

"And the most exciting news of the week is that I saw a story online that said *Chase and Corbin* are doing a reunion show. It's supposed to be a limited series."

I rolled my eyes and chuckled.

"*That's* as big as you killing it at Cambridge?"

"Mom, you know how much I love that show."

"Oh I know. The walls of your room are still covered with posters."

"I took some of them down."

"Yeah, the ones of Chase."

She scrunched her nose.

"You know I've always been a Corbin girl."

The show is about two brothers. One was portrayed as the high school stud while his stepbrother was chubby and awkward. Grace had a crush on the latter.

"So how's the book coming along?" she asked when she was telling me the details of the article that may or may not be true. It felt like I was having a conversation with middle-school Grace again.

"I'm almost done. I just have two more chapters to write. Three with the bonus epilogue."

"Mom, that's so awesome! I'm so glad Aunt Winnie convinced you to go to Seaside. The change of space really helped." She narrowed her eyes and studied my face. "Unless there's something else going on there in Seaside. A little *romance* maybe?"

"Why do you say that?"

"I don't know." She shrugged. "There's just something there. A twinkle, a glow, a blush," she said with dramatic flair. "You're the romance author, help me out here."

I still haven't mentioned Max to her. Yes, she's an adult, but she's also my daughter. Since I expected Max to be a summer fling, I didn't see a reason to tell her about him. But now that we've spent so much time together, chances are I'll say something about him when telling her about my time here. Plus I have tons of pictures of him. Obviously I could hide them, but why should I?

"There is a man I've been seeing."

"Mom! Writing and dating? Seaside *has* been good for you. Maybe you should stay longer."

I shook my head.

"This isn't my real life. I have to get back home."

"Why?" Before I could think of an answer, she said, "How many writers do you know

that have moved for an extended period of time? Or sold all their belongings, bought an RV, and hit the road."

There've been a lot, that's for sure. One nice thing about being a full-time writer is that you can do it anywhere.

I heard Aunt Winnie walking up the stairs and took it as an opportunity to change the subject.

"Hold on," I said to Grace just before I stood and headed to the door. I opened it just as my aunt stepped on the upstairs landing. "Aunt Winnie, Grace is on FaceTime. Come in and say hello."

I thought about what Grace said as the two chatted. I'll admit the thought of staying another few weeks has crossed my mind. I wonder how Max will feel about that. Not that he owns the town of Seaside, but still. We've been spending so much time together. Would he feel obligated for this to continue or would it just stop if I stayed longer?

"It was so nice talking to you. Good night."

"Good night, Aunt Winnie."

Thankfully I got out of my head long enough to hear that exchange. Aunt Winnie stood and squeezed my arm.

"I'm going out to dinner," she said. "So I'll see you later."

I sat back behind the desk and said good night to Grace.

"Think about what I said," she said.

"I will."

"I'm serious."

"So am I."

It's not like I have to make a decision tonight. I'm not scheduled to leave for another three weeks. Hopefully by then I'll figure out what to do.

MAX

"HOW WAS YOUR DAY?" I ASKED AFTER GREETING EVE WITH A kiss.

"It was wonderful. I typed 'The End' on my manuscript."

I picked her up and spun her around then set her down on the sand.

"That's amazing."

She placed her hand on her chest and looked up at me.

"You have no idea how relieved I feel. I was so stuck for so long..." She trailed off and shook her head. "I have to do a final read-through but after that, it's off to my editor."

"I'm so happy for you."

I put my arm around her shoulders and pulled her close to kiss the top of her head, then held her hand as we walked down the beach toward my place. We have a couple things to talk about and I figured a quiet night in would be perfect for an important conversation. Normally I'd just pick her up, but tonight I suggested meeting on the beach and taking a slow stroll.

We talked about the book she'd just written and all the ones she's published. When I looked her up online, I was impressed with her extensive catalog. I'm not much of a reader, but I do plan to read one of her books at some point.

"So what's next?" I asked. "Will you take a break?"

"I'll probably jump into the next book. You know, strike while the iron's hot."

As we approached the steps to my deck, Eve looked around.

"God I'll miss this view," she said.

I hadn't planned on discussing this until we were sitting down to dinner. But I can't ignore the fact that she just gave me the perfect opening.

"Not if you don't leave."

She looked at me, eyes wide.

"What do you mean?"

"Why don't you stay a while longer?" She just blinked so I continued. "I'd love to spend more time with you."

"Um…"

Her eyes shifted toward the ocean then back at me, but she didn't say anything else. I pushed a few strands of hair that escaped her ponytail behind her ear.

"We can discuss it more after dinner." I held out my hand. "Come on."

Throughout dinner we talked about everything but her staying in Seaside. But once she was fed and relaxing in an Adirondack chair enjoying the view, I figured it was time to bring up the topic again.

"I could tell I shocked you by what I said before."

"A little bit."

"Have you thought about staying longer?"

"Sort of. I'll admit the idea was in the back of my head, but I didn't really seriously consider it until my daughter mentioned it on our FaceTime call."

"Is she for or against you staying?"

"Definitely for. She said Seaside has been good for me."

"I agree," I said with a smile. "So what are your thoughts on staying?"

"As long as Aunt Winnie doesn't mind, I could stay." She frowned. "Although, I guess I could get an Airbnb."

"Or you could stay here." Her eyes widened. "With me."

She stared at me for several heartbeats.

"You'd want me to stay here with you?" I nodded. "Wow."

"Is that a good *wow*?"

"It's good. Surprised, but good."

"Why surprised?"

"I don't know. This was just supposed to be a summer thing and then–"

She shook her head. I waited for her to complete the sentence, but when she didn't, I finished it with my own words.

"Then I fell in love with you."

"You..."

"I fell in love with you." I shifted off my chair to kneel in front of her. Taking her hands in mine, I looked her in the eye. "I love you Eve. Please say you'll stay."

CHAPTER 16

Eve

"I'm feeling all the feels," Anjannette said. "I'm thrilled that you're getting your own

happily-ever-after, but I miss you being here."

My pole peeps couldn't Zoom last week so they're just finding out I'm extending my trip. I could have texted them, but wanted to share all the details. Well not *all*, just the non-sexy parts.

"It's not exactly a happily-ever-after just yet," I said. "We're just hanging out, seeing where things go."

"Eve," Sophie said. "The man asked you to stay, told you he loved you, and wants you to move in with him. I'd say that's pretty damn close to every HEA I've ever written."

"You guys are doing so much more than hanging out," Keera said. "He's obviously crazy about you."

"It's all so surreal. I never thought anything like this would ever happen to me."

"What did Grace say? And your parents?" Anjannette asked.

"Grace is fine with it. She's happy I'm both writing and dating again. My parents..." I shrugged. "I'm guessing they think I'm having a mid-life crisis."

"You're finally living for you instead of everyone else," Sophie said. "Enjoy."

"So are you going to stay with Max or your aunt?" Keera asked.

"I've split this past week between the two. Max and I have a good thing going right now. I don't want to mess it up by moving too fast," I said. "By the time John and I moved in together, we'd been dating almost two years and spent most of our time together, but it was still an adjustment. Since I have the option, I'll just take this thing with Max one day at a time."

"Or one night as the case may be." Anjannette bobbed her eyebrows.

"Okay, enough about me," I said. "Fill me in on all the studio gossip."

I really do want to hear about everything that's happening, but it's also a way to switch the conversation away from Max and me. As they filled me in, my emotions were like a rollercoaster. It's nice to keep updated but it hurts my heart too. Part of me wants to be there, living my well-ordered life. But another part of me knows that now that I've spread my wings, I won't be satisfied with the status quo.

"I miss you guys so much." Their images blurred as I blinked away tears. "I wish you could all come visit."

"Road trip!" Keera yelled.

"Or maybe just take a plane. Three thousand miles makes for a long road trip." I turned my attention to Anjannette. "Although Seattle is only a couple hundred miles away so if you're ever going there with Leo, let me know and I'll come meet you." I shook my head. "Now *I'm* getting ahead of myself. I extended my trip a month, not ten years."

"For *now*," Anjannette said.

"Just relax and enjoy getting to know your hottie handyman better," Sophie said. "We're here for you whenever you need us."

"I love you guys."

They each said, "I love you too."

No amount of blinking held off the tears after that.

MAX

THE MUSIC PAUSED AS MY PHONE RANG FOR THE TENTH TIME IN the past hour. Yes, the tenth.

"That your mother again?"

Since she has her own ringtone now, I didn't have to look at my caller ID to confirm that it's definitely her.

"Yep."

"Are you ever gonna answer?"

"Nope."

Today we're replacing the front and back doors on the Weaver cabin. The structure is super crooked, so the job is taking longer than planned. It's the only thing we're doing today so at least it's not putting us behind schedule on anything else.

"You know she's stubborn."

"I wonder where she gets that from."

Pop can be stubborn as hell, which can make him tough to deal with, but it's also the reason we even know each other. My mother got pregnant with me when she was eighteen and followed her baby daddy to Los Angeles. I've never met my father, so that tells you how well that went. Even though that's true, she didn't come back to Seaside. Ever.

I only have a relationship with Pop because he'd come pick me up and bring me here for a couple weeks every summer. Through those visits and random phone calls, we got to know each other. Which is why he was the person I reached out to when I needed to get out.

"She'll just keep callin'."

I finished adding shims and grabbed the level. It looks pretty good, but I stepped back for Pop to check.

"And I'll keep ignoring her," I said. "Eventually I'll just block her."

He shook his head and muttered something under his breath.

"Pop, she only wants to try to talk me into doing that reunion show. If I thought it was anything else, I'd answer."

"Your mother and me aren't the only ones that are stubborn."

"Guilty as charged."

I nailed the door into place and stepped back while Pop opened and closed it a couple times.

"Looks good," he said. "You don't even need me anymore."

Truth be told, I haven't needed him for things like this for quite a few years, but I didn't say that. Pop has been making similar comments more often these days. It makes me wonder if he's getting ready to retire.

Logically I know there will be a day when Pop isn't around, but it's not something I like to think about. Like he said last time we had this conversation, he and my mom are all I have. Once he's gone, my mom will be my only living relative. That's a pretty depressing thought.

"So Eve is stayin' longer."

"Yep, another month."

"So she was okay with all that?" he asked, gesturing toward my phone.

"I haven't told her yet."

His grunt said more than any words could.

"I'll do it tonight."

I've said that before but always seem to get sidetracked. But I know that I have to tell her. If not tonight, then definitely tomorrow.

My phone buzzed and I walked over to check the text message. Eve's name on the screen brightened my thoughts. Maybe if our conversation goes well, she'll stay in my life a lot longer.

CHAPTER 17

Eve

I PEEKED MY EYES OPEN AND LOOKED AROUND THE ROOM. IF the masculine decor didn't tell me where I'm waking up today, the hot man spooning me from behind would. As planned, I've been splitting the past week between Max's place and Aunt Winnie's. So far it's working well.

"Good morning."

His gravelly voice vibrated against my ear.

"Good morning."

I wiggled against the erection that's poking at my ass. He slid his hand up and cupped my breast.

"Keep doing that and you'll be in trouble."

"Mmm, seems I like trouble these days."

I've never slept naked, but when I'm with Max, it seems natural. Besides, it makes morning sex a lot easier.

Max dragged his hand down to slip between my thighs. I pressed my leg back and draped it over his hip offering better access. He didn't need another invitation.

It's amazing how well this man knows my body after just a couple months. His fingers circled and plucked, stroked and plunged, bringing me to the edge of orgasm in a short amount of time. He thrust his hips forward, pressing against me from behind and creating a mind-blowing rhythm as he stroked my clit.

"*Max.*" He always makes sure I come at least once before plunging into me, but today I don't want to wait. "I want to come with you. *Now.*"

He rolled onto his back and pulled me with him. We'd stopped using condoms a few weeks ago so I straddled his hips and sat, impaling myself on his hard cock. Our matching groans echoed through the room when I was fully seated and started to move.

Normally I'd take it slow and tease him, but that's when I've already had the edge taken off. Right now, I have one goal in mind and that's to ride us hard and fast to orgasm.

Sitting back, I pressed him even deeper inside me. He moved his hands up to pluck at my nipples. That did it. I felt the ripples start deep inside and I moved faster then faster still, urging them on until the sensation engulfed my entire body. Max dug his fingers into my ass and held me tight as he thrust up twice then groaned his completion.

I rested my head against his chest and listened as his heartbeat returned to normal. My stomach growled and I bounced up and down with his chuckle.

"I guess it's time to feed you," he said.

"I'll cook breakfast." Sitting back to look him in the eye, I added, "I owe you a meal or two."

I shifted off him and stood. He turned onto his back with his hands resting behind his head.

"And I'll be a man of leisure, lying here until breakfast is served."

After giving him a quick kiss, I headed to the bathroom to clean up and slip into his robe. I never thought I'd be so comfortable with another man after my divorce, but things are just natural between Max and me. From the moment I laid eyes on him, I felt like I knew him. Maybe we met in a past life.

I walked into the kitchen and perused the cupboards and refrigerator.

"Eggs, pancakes, or French toast?" I yelled.

"Eggs sound good. Over easy. And lots of toast."

I'd just cracked the eggs into the pan when I heard a pounding on the front door. The one leading from the workshop that I've never used.

"Max!" More pounding. "Open the door. I know you're in there."

He ran out of the bedroom, slipping his legs into shorts along the way. It would have been comical if I didn't have a feeling of dread in the pit of my stomach.

Max opened the door and a woman marched through. Even in four-inch stilettos, she's not as tall as me.

"What are you doing *here*?"

"I've been blowing up your phone and you haven't answered," she said. "Obviously I need to talk to you. *That's* what I'm doing here."

"I don't have anything to say to you and I definitely don't want to hear what you have to say."

I stood frozen in place, wearing Max's robe, my hair in a messy bun, and holding the spatula in front of me. In contrast, the mystery woman's bleach blonde hair is styled into a chin-length bob that falls right back into place after every head shake. Her flawless red lipstick matches her nail polish perfectly. She can't be more than five-feet-four in heels, but exudes power, giving her a larger-than-life presence.

"This is a great opportunity."

"I don't care."

"They're offering a *lot* of money."

"Again. I. Don't. Care."

Max walked over and took the spatula from my hand, removed the eggs from the burner, and turned off the stove.

"It's been twelve years, don't you think you're being ridiculous?"

He turned to face her, holding onto the countertop behind him with a death grip.

"Mom, I don't want to act anymore. I like my life here and don't want that messed up."

Mom?

At least it's not a long-lost girlfriend or wife.

A slow smirk crossed the woman's face and I knew whatever was going to come out of her mouth would *not* be good.

"One phone call from me and your so-called *life* will be turned upside down."

"You're *threatening* me? *Seriously*?"

She shrugged.

"Call it incentivizing."

"Why? Don't you have enough active clients to keep your bank account full?"

"Why?" She snorted. "Max, *Chase and Corbin* is one of the most successful, not to mention profitable, shows the network has ever aired. And a whole new audience has fallen in love with it through syndication."

They continued spitting words at each other, but I have no idea what was being said. *Chase and Corbin* kept spinning through my mind like the reruns Max's mother just mentioned. I looked at the man I've been involved with for the past few months, seeing him with new eyes.

That's when I saw it. Sucking a sharp breath, I placed my hand over my mouth.

"Oh my God, you're Corbin Kendrick."

They stopped talking and looked over at me.

"Eve."

Max reached out to touch me but I dodged out of the way and headed toward the door. He started to follow me but I held up my hand, stopping his steps.

"Please don't."

MAX

"ARE YOU HAPPY NOW?"

I turned to face my mother and she didn't really seem to care. I'm not sure why I thought she would. The woman has ice in her veins.

"Oh please, there's no way she didn't know."

"Not everyone has ulterior motives like you."

"Yeah, just like that girl you dated when you were eighteen."

"Eve is different." She snorted and I shook my head. "I'm not talking about her with you, and I'm not discussing a reunion show. It's not happening or if it does, I won't be in it."

"Max, who's car is in the driveway?"

Pop's voice carried up the stairs a second before I heard his footsteps. The man rarely loses his game face, but he couldn't hide his shock at seeing my mother.

"Hi dad," she said.

"Tally." His eyes shifted between us. "What are you doing here?"

"Max and I had something to discuss and he wasn't answering his phone."

"Must be pretty important. You haven't stepped foot in Seaside in more than three decades."

"Just offering him an opportunity he can't refuse."

"But let me guess, he did refuse."

"He did, but I'm confident I can convince him."

The two were talking as if I wasn't here, like they used to do when I was a child. Before Pop could answer, I spoke.

"You won't convince me. I haven't wanted to be a part of that world since I was fifteen."

"Max, it's *one* show."

"It's a *limited series*. For now."

She didn't deny that so I'm guessing that if this limited series they're planning does well, they'll want another one. Or God forbid, plan a whole reboot like so many shows are doing nowadays.

"I can't talk to you when you're being so unreasonable," she said. "I'm staying at The Seaside Hotel. Call me when you're ready to talk."

I was about to tell her that will never happen, but there's nothing my mother likes more than a challenge. So I kept quiet just so she'd leave. She disappeared down the stairs and a few seconds later, I heard her pull out of the driveway.

"I told you ya should've answered the phone."

Rubbing my hand against the back of my neck, I fought to get my temper under control. I don't want to lash out at Pop. He's not the source of my aggravation.

"She would have just showed up anyway when I didn't agree to do what she wants."

His answering grunt told me he agreed.

"So what are you gonna do now?"

"I don't know." I looked around my apartment. "If she tells everyone where I am, it's gonna get crazy here for a while."

"What about with Eve?"

"I don't know about that either." I looked over at him. "What *can* I do?"

He shook his head.

"I'm not an expert with women, but it seems to me you need to give her some time to cool off," he said. "Then go tell her everything you should have said at the beginning of the summer."

As far as an *I told you so*, that's pretty mild.

"I'm gonna take a shower, then I'll head over to Winnie's to see if Eve will talk to me."

"I think you should give the girl more time. How about we go out to breakfast and *then* you go to Winnie's?"

CHAPTER 18

Eve

"Why didn't you tell me?" I asked for at least the fifth time.

"It wasn't my story to tell," she said. "Besides, I didn't think it would matter."

"Wouldn't matter? Aunt Winnie, I handled the fact that he's eight years younger than me. Now I find out he's the person my daughter had a crush on." I let out a sarcastic chuckle. "*Has* a crush on. She was just talking about the reunion show the other night." I wiped the tears from my cheeks with a crumbled tissue then blew my nose. "Besides, don't you think that's something he should have told me? I mean, I've been an open book."

"I'll admit he should have told you," she said, running her hand over my back in long soothing strokes. "But should the fact that he didn't be a deal breaker?"

"Maybe it *shouldn't*, but it makes me wonder what else he isn't telling me. And what kind of things will he choose not to tell me in the future?" I shook my head. "I can't live in a relationship full of secrets again."

My phone buzzed and I looked down to find a Zoom link. I'd sent my pole ladies a *911* text and within an hour they put a call together. Talk about true friends.

"Go talk to your friends," Aunt Winnie said. "I'll be here when you come back down."

I walked up the steps, my legs feeling like lead. My friends were already on Zoom when I pulled up the app.

"Well there goes *that* theory," Keera said.

"What theory?" I asked

"I hoped you were calling to tell us you got engaged or something. But based on your face, I'd say that's not the case."

There are women who cry with dignity. Tears gracefully cascade down their cheeks and just the tip of their nose gets red. I am not one of those women. With my blotchy face, swollen eyes, and runny nose, I could win an ugly crier contest.

Avoiding my image on the screen, I alternated focusing on Anjannette, Keera, and Sophie as I spoke.

"No engagement. In fact, the relationship is over."

Those words brought a fresh rush of tears. Like the good friends they are, the ladies waited for me to gain my composure and start speaking again.

"I found out this morning that Max is Corbin Kendrick."

"*What?*"

That single word radiated from my computer's speaker in three distinct voices. I would have laughed if I wasn't feeling so miserable.

"And he never told me. His mother showed up and started a whole thing. I'm guessing she is, or at least *was*, his agent."

I relayed the events of this morning, finishing with the part when I walked out the door and stormed down the beach wearing nothing but his robe.

"Have you talked to him?" Anjannette asked. "Let him explain?"

"What's there to explain? He could have told me at any point the past several weeks, but didn't."

"Maybe he had a good reason." This from Keera.

I rubbed my temples.

"Like what?"

"I don't know," she said.

"Seriously?"

"Eve, you've been happier with Max than I've seen you in the past ten years," Sophie said. "Don't let that go over a misunderstanding."

"Is that what this is?" That question came out more like a screech and I took a breath to rein it in. "A simple misunderstanding?"

"I don't know that it's simple, but in the grand scheme of things yeah, I'd call it a misunderstanding," she said.

I shifted my gaze among the three of them.

"So you think I'm being unreasonable."

"No, we're not saying that," Anjannette said. She looked around and the others nodded. "What I think we're saying is that you should give him a chance to explain. Don't judge him based on your past experience. It's not fair, honey."

Part of me knows she has a point, but the hurt part wants to wallow a little while longer.

"I'll think about that," I said. "Thanks for putting this call together so fast."

"You've jumped on at least a hundred 911 calls for us through the years. It's time for payback," Keera said.

"Now call Grace and tell her so that you can put *that*

issue out of your head," Sophie said. "Yes, he was her celebrity crush, but he's so much more to you. I'm sure she'll be cool about it."

Grace is a great kid, but this seems too weird to be *cool* about.

I said goodbye to the ladies and shut down Zoom. Picking up my phone, I texted Grace and asked her to call as soon as she could. Seconds later, FaceTime rang.

MAX

WINNIE WAS SITTING ON THE BACK PORCH WHEN I ARRIVED. I'D expected her to freeze me out, but she patted the seat next to her. I took her invitation and sat, unsure what to say. So I went with the first thing that came to mind.

"I should have told her."

She nodded.

"Maybe not immediately, but yes, once you got more involved, you definitely should have mentioned it."

"I'm surprised you didn't tell her."

"It wasn't my story to tell."

"I guess not." Resting my hands on the table, I leaned forward. "So what should I do now?"

"Talk to her, explain things."

"Do you think she'll listen?"

Winnie looked out at the ocean and I didn't think she was going to respond. But thankfully, finally, she did.

"She's not an unreasonable person, so I think she'll listen," she said. "Whether or not she forgives you is another question."

"I really screwed up, didn't I?" I dragged my fingers through my hair, wishing I could go back in time and make this right. "But honestly, I didn't think it was that big a deal. All that happened so long ago. That's not me anymore."

"Do you know why Eve's marriage ended?" I nodded. "So this may not be that big a deal to someone else, and you're right, it did happen a long time ago. You're not that person anymore." She placed her hand over mine and squeezed. "But to Eve, none of that matters. What matters is that you lied to her. True it was a lie of omission, but it translates to the same thing. Her ex-husband had a whole other life going on for years, so anything you keep from her is going to be an issue."

"Put that way, it makes so much sense."

"Talk to her, explain your position, and let her process."

"For how long?"

"As long as it takes."

The back door opened and I glanced over my shoulder to find a tear-stained Eve looking at Winnie, eyes wide. I took it as a good sign when she stood in the doorway instead of going back inside.

"I'll leave you two alone to talk," Winnie said as she stood and breezed past me.

Eve stepped onto the porch, letting her aunt go inside.

"Can we talk?" I asked.

She hesitated for a second but finally walked over and sat in the chair Winnie just vacated. She didn't say anything, so I continued.

"Pop kept urging me to tell you about my past." I shrugged. "I did plan on telling you, but I didn't think it was that big a deal. But now I understand that anything other than complete and total honesty is a problem."

"Why didn't you just tell me?" she asked. "I blabbed on and on about marriage and family."

"You know, a lot of people go through awkward teenage years, and when they're through them, they burn their yearbooks and swear their family to secrecy," I said. "But my awkward teen years are in reruns."

I let her process that for a minute before telling her about my mom, and how I ended up starring in one of the most popular teen shows of its time.

"With no experience or education, she somehow talked her way into a job at a talent agent's office. She made herself indispensable and eventually started getting me booked for commercials."

"How old were you?"

"Two, almost three."

"Eventually I got small parts in sitcoms and when the concept for *Chase and Corbin* came along, she pushed hard for me to read."

"Did you enjoy it?"

"At first I didn't mind, but once I got older, I hated it. Instead of going to school, I had a tutor and I felt so isolated. It got to the point that I only spent time with the cast and my mother when she was home."

"Did you tell her?"

"You met her today. Do you think she'd listen to a child?"

"I guess not."

"She signed a four-year contract for me right before my eighteenth birthday. I'm sure I could have gotten a lawyer and contested it, but I figured I'd play nice. I told them I was out when my contract was up. The show was still successful so they thought I'd keep doing it. But once I turned twenty-one, I was done."

"And you came here?"

"I came here."

I explained how Pop stayed in my life through the years and offered me a place to live and work.

"How have you stayed anonymous here for so long?"

"At first, I didn't have a car or bills or anything in my name. So even though people could search the internet for my real name, it wouldn't have led them anywhere."

She chuckled, which I took as a good sign.

"You know how I kept saying you look familiar?" He nodded. "That's because my daughter was obsessed with you. Kind of still is."

"With *me*?"

"When all her friends went on and on about Chase, she only had eyes for you. Posters of you are still on the walls of her room and she watched the show so much, I probably know all your lines."

"But I felt connected to you too, so I think there's just something between us."

"Maybe." She shrugged. "Either way, it freaked me out when I realized you didn't tell me something so big. It made me wonder what else you're hiding."

I drew a cross over my heart with my right hand

"I swear, this is it. There's nothing else to tell."

She looked down and traced her finger along the edge of the table. Without looking up, she said, "I need total honesty if we're going to continue this."

"You have it. I swear, you have it. Just please give me another chance."

As soon as she nodded, I was out of my chair and on my knees in front of her. Placing my hands on either side of her face, I drew her mouth down for a soft kiss to seal our second chance.

When I pulled back, she nibbled on her bottom lip and studied me.

"What are you going to do about your mother?"

I sat back in my seat and pulled her out of hers and onto my lap. She rested her head on my shoulder.

"I'm not doing the reunion show. If she tells people where I am, I'll deal with it. We'll deal with it together."

Her smile curled against my chest just before she pushed back to meet my gaze.

"Regardless of what your mother does or doesn't do, you're going to have to meet some rabid fans," she said. "My daughter and pole friends expect an introduction soon. And since I met your mom, it's only fair you meet my parents."

"Yeah?"

She nodded.

"Yeah."

"I love you, Everly Reese."

"And I love you Max Corbin."

EPILOGUE

Eve

Three months later…

"Grace is going to freak when she sees this."

I held up my left hand, admiring the cushion-cut diamond Max had placed on it two nights ago.

"You don't think she suspected?"

"*I* didn't suspect it," I said. "In case that wasn't clear."

"If you did, you're a pretty good actress."

When Max proposed, I cried so hard I hyperventilated and almost passed out.

"I honestly didn't expect a proposal."

"We've been discussing how we're going to split our time between coasts. You don't think I'd expect you to make an honest man of me to do that?"

I laughed at both the earnest look on his face and the old-fashioned phrase.

"Are you nervous about meeting everyone?"

"No, since we've been Zooming and Facetiming, I feel like I know them already. Meeting in person is just icing on the cake."

We're flying to Scranton so everyone can finally meet Max and to celebrate Christmas. We'd tried to go sooner, but Grace couldn't swing a trip home before now, and I didn't want her to be the last one to meet him.

"I hope they got the shock of you out of their systems so they don't act like total fools," I said.

"It's okay if they do because I'll probably embarrass myself when I meet Leo Marakis."

"Leo's just a normal guy like you."

"Still, he's one of my favorite baseball players. He doesn't even play for my team, but I've followed him for years."

"It's kind of funny," I said. "Anjannette is engaged to a Major League ballplayer and I'm engaged to a Hollywood star. What are the chances?"

"*Former* Hollywood star."

I shrugged.

"Po-ta-to, po-tah-to."

Max's mother made good on her threat and gave an interview exposing where he lives. She even included a new picture. I wouldn't say his fans swarmed to Seaside, but they definitely showed up. For the most part, they've been respectful of his time and privacy. They just want an autograph or selfie and then they leave him alone.

The reporters were a little more difficult to shake, but eventually left when they had other stories to follow. Or as Max says, "They left when they realized how boring my life is."

"I don't know why my mother thought telling people where I live would convince me to do a reunion show."

"I don't know either, but be forewarned, you're going to have at least five people trying to convince you to do it in Scranton."

"They've already been trying, especially Sophie."

"More than the reunion show, Sophie wants me to write *our* story and have you star in the movie version," I said. "She's just so thrilled that she's the one who predicted it."

"That is kind of funny."

"It seems our relationship is a Hallmark Movie cliché," I said. "The blocked writer and the hot handyman."

"You're not blocked anymore."

"No, not since you 'got my juices flowing again,' as Sophie says."

"I really can't wait to meet your friends," he said.

I thought about that final night with my friends all those months ago and shook my head.

"I still can't believe this is my life." I blinked until his image wasn't blurry. "Before I left for Seaside, I told my friends that nothing romantic ever happens in my life. And then I got there and the *most* romantic thing happened. I fell in love with you."

He wiped a tear that had escaped from my cheek and smiled.

"And I fell in love with you."

Leaning forward, he kissed me, then pulled me into his arms.

The captain announced that he was beginning to descend toward Scranton. When I left the city six months ago, I was a divorced romance author with writers' block. Now I'm heading home with three new books written and a brand-new fiancé. Sometimes life really is better than fiction.

Join my newsletter to stay up to date on me and my books.

Check out Sophie and Jamie's story...

Chapter 1

. . .

Sophie

"I can't believe you're here!" Throwing my arms around Eve, I tugged her through the front door and into a tight hug. "I've missed you so much."

"Don't mind us," Anjannette said. "We'll just stand out here and freeze."

Still holding onto Eve, I backed into the house, allowing Anjannette and Keera to enter. I pulled back just far enough to see her face.

"I can't believe you're here," I said again.

"I know. It kind of feels like I've been away forever."

"That's because you have."

She chuckled.

"It's only been a few months."

"Eight," I said. "It's been *eight* months."

"I know. I planned on being here for Christmas, but then my whole family decided to come out to Seaside for the holidays."

"I get it, but I really missed you."

"Don't mind Keera and me over here," Anjannette said from the dining room. "We'll just amuse ourselves and eat all this food."

I released Eve then we both walked over to the dining room. Anjanette and Keera had brought pizza and wings and set the table with the paper plates and napkins the restaurant provided.

"Nice of you to join us."

I grabbed a slice and looked over at Anjannette.

"There's no need to be dramatic," I said.

"Dramatic?" she placed her hand against her chest *dramatically*. "Moi?"

"Always."

She shrugged, then took a big bite of pizza.

"So tell us everything that's been going on with you and Max," Keera said to Eve.

"You act like you don't grill me for details during our Zoom calls."

"It's not the same." Keera shook her head. "We like you in the same room."

"Not that we're not thrilled that you've found true love out there on the left coast," Anjannette added.

Keera pointed between Eve and me with a chicken wing.

"And if one of you doesn't write *that* story, I'm gonna scream."

Eve's trip to visit her aunt in Seaside, Oregon last summer resulted in her falling in love with the local handyman and moving to the idyllic coastal town. The fact that said handyman is not only nine years younger but also happens to be the former child star of one of the hottest TV shows from the last decade makes their story that much more interesting.

I spread my arms out wide and pointed at myself.

"Not to brag, but I am the one who predicted her life would imitate a Hallmark Channel movie before she went out there."

"Then write the damn story," Keera said.

"I think Eve needs to do it. It would be great for marketing."

"Yeah, but that would be icky. Even though it'd be fiction, readers would think I'd opened the door to our bedroom."

"You say that like it's a bad thing."

Keera bobbed her eyebrows and Eve threw a crumpled napkin at her forehead.

"Besides, Max and I are old news. Keera and Simon are the new kids on the block. Not to mention the fact that Anjannette and Leo are engaged and planning a huge wedding."

"Even if we just included Leo's immediate family, the wedding would be huge."

I finished two slices and a handful of wings as Anjannette filled Eve in on her latest adventures in wedding planning. I half listened since I've already heard some of it. Leo is from a big Greek family and they're trying to get married without having to rent an arena to fit all the guests.

It's funny, when I started taking pole dance lessons at the studio, Anjannette had sworn off men, Keera was healing a broken heart by dating *dick band-aids*...her words, not mine... and Eve and I were both newly divorced. Now the three of them are in healthy, happy relationships.

"But enough about me," Anjannette said. "Sophie is the one living the *Sex and the City* life. Hearing about that is more interesting than listening to my guest list woes."

"I told you guys that I'm done with the dating scene."

"Yeah, but we didn't think you were serious," Keera said.

"Oh, I'm serious."

"You were having fun *exploring*." Eve said. "Did something happen?"

She looked alarmed as she asked that question and I quickly reassured her.

"No, it just stopped being fun."

"I get that," Keera said. "It turns into a grind after a while."

I finished my wine and set the glass down, keeping my fingers wrapped around the stem.

"Rob was the only person I had sex with and after the divorce, I was kind of like a kid in a candy store. But after a while, I wasn't enjoying it anymore." I circled my pointer finger around the rim of the glass as I collected my thoughts. "I even checked out those BDSM clubs, but it only made me realize that lifestyle isn't for me." I shifted my gaze between the three of them. "So I'm done with dating. I'm better off on my own."

Keera and Anjannette shared a look then burst out laughing.

"Famous last words," Anjannette said.

"Yeah, you know both of us took a man break and then Leo walked into her life and I rediscovered Simon in a whole new way."

I shook my head.

"I was married for twenty years. I'm not looking for a relationship."

They all nodded, but the looks on their faces said I'd eat those last words as soon as the perfect man walked into my life. Especially Eve's since she said the same thing last year.

"I'm serious," I said. "Been there, done that, and have written many books."

"Good one," Keera said.

"Thanks, I pride myself on my wordmanship." I popped the last bite of crust into my mouth and chewed, debating on whether I want to share my next thought. As I swallowed, I decided I did. "There is one thing I'd love that I didn't get while I was *exploring.*"

"What's that?" Eve asked.

"Amazing sex." Three sets of rounded eyes just stared at me. "What?"

"You didn't get that with *any* of the guys you were with?" Anjannette asked.

"You say *any* as if I banged the whole third fleet," I said. "I was pretty selective about who I spent time with and I only had sex with the few guys that made me tingly in all the right places." I shook my head. "Unfortunately, none of them lived up to those tingles."

Keera leaned forward, resting her elbow against the table, and held up one finger.

"Not one?"

"Nope." I sighed. "A couple were better than the others, and one had a few moves I enjoyed. But honestly, not one of them gave me an orgasm better than I can give myself."

"Damn."

Anjannette punctuated that single word by picking up her glass and finishing her wine in one gulp.

"And the thing is...how do you know? They walk the walk and talk the talk, and then..." I made a raspberry sound and gave a thumb's down.

"The struggle is real, my friend. Honestly, I don't think I've ever been with a guy who didn't need training." A slow smile spread across Anjannette's face. "Well, except for Leo."

"Which is why you're putting a ring on it," I said. "But I'm not lying when I say I don't want anything serious." I took in a breath and let it out. "You know what I really want?"

"I think this is going to be good," Eve said in a stage whisper then leaned toward me, and smirked. "What do you want?"

"I want a man to take me out to a nice dinner, bring me home, fuck me hard...preferably with multiple mind-blowing orgasms...then go away until the next week. A true friend with benefits. Hell, we can even skip the *friends* part as long as the chemistry is there and he satisfies the afore-mentioned requirements." I held out my hands. "You'd think I'd be every man's fantasy, wouldn't you?"

"You'd think," Anjannette said.

"That sounds logical to me," Keera said. "But Granny Vi always said that at a certain point, men either want a nurse or purse. Meaning they want a woman to take care of them or to support them."

"I am so using that in my next book," Eve said. "I'll give Granny Vi full credit, of course."

"She'll be thrilled."

"Maybe I need to have Granny Vi pick a man for me. She's proven her ability to predict dick size. Maybe she can take one look and know if a guy is a dud or a stud in the sack."

"I'll ask if she wants to be your wing woman."

"In the meantime, until I can find a man who will give me what I can't give myself, I'll stay solo."

****

Jamie

"You could help, you know."

"But you're doing such a great job all by yourself," Elliot said from his perch on the black velvet sofa across the room. "I don't want to mess up your system."

"My *system* is putting paint on the roller and pushing it against the wall."

"You're better at it than I am."

I climbed down the portable scaffolding, unlocked the wheels, and pushed it to the other side of the wall.

"I did all the trim. All you need to do is get off your ass, pick up a roller, and start painting."

Out of the corner of my eye, I saw him stick his tongue

out at me as he stood. I shook my head and leaned down to lock the wheels, then climbed back up.

"Know what I think?"

"Not really, but I'm sure you'll tell me anyway."

"You need to get laid," he said. "That's why you're cranky."

"I'm not cranky."

"Yeah you are. You're cranky and grumpy."

"I'm not. I just want to finish renovating *your* studio. I need you to help if you want it ready for your training class."

"It's not my fault I'm not good at this stuff."

"Spare me," I said. "Growing up, we worked side-by-side with your dad doing *this stuff*."

"It's just not my thing." He looked up at me and smiled. "That's what I have you for."

I shook my head and went back to the task at hand. I'm starving and I want to finish this first coat before stopping for lunch.

Behind me, I heard Elliott shuffling around. A quick glance over my shoulder confirmed that he'd finally started to paint.

If I'm being totally honest, when he asked me to help him renovate the pole studio, I didn't really expect him to pitch in. I just like to bust his ass.

"Do you like this color?"

Squeezing the handle of my roller until my knuckles turned white, I ignored the question and kept painting, hoping Elliott would let it go. But history has taught me that he wouldn't, and history is rarely wrong.

"Jamie. Jame. Jamie."

Taking in a calming breath, I slowly let it out and turned around.

"There's no need to say my name three times. You sound like Sheldon from the *Big Bang Theory*."

"You weren't answering."

"What do you want?"

"Do you like this color?"

"Yeah, it looks great."

He scrunched his nose.

"You think?"

"I do, which is why I said it."

Backing up to the middle of the room, he turned in a circle.

"I don't know." He gestured with the roller. "It looks kind of...blah."

"You're just used to the walls being Pepto Bismol pink."

"Hmmm."

Cocking his head to the side, he studied the wall he'd just painted.

There's no way in hell I'm repainting. With these high ceilings, the trim took forever and doing the top half has been a pain in the ass.

"Don't start second-guessing your choices. The burgundy and gold look good, especially with the exposed brick wall."

Elliott narrowed his eyes.

"The colors are *copper red* and *anjou pear*."

"Whatever. You're looking at one coat with the sun and all the lights bouncing off it."

He shrugged.

"Maybe."

He'd been planning this renovation for months and it took him longer to pick out the paint than make any other decision. I figured I'd have to do more convincing, but surprisingly, he went back to the task at hand.

With both of us working, the walls were completely covered within a half hour. It took another ten minutes to get cleaned up and within fifteen we were walking through the front door of Saucy Girls Pizza.

Saucy Girl #1, Gina Romano, waved as we sat at our favorite table in the corner. She approached a minute later and set a Diet Coke in front of Elliott and handed me an unsweetened iced tea. Being a regular has its privileges.

"Having the usual?" she asked.

"Yes," I said. "And I'll have an antipasto salad, too."

"We'll take two plates with that salad," Elliott said.

Normally I'd tell him I'm not sharing, but the salad in question is big enough to feed a family of four, and I don't want to watch him pout.

"Got it. Cara is just finishing up a big takeout order, but she'll get on this asap," she said, referring to her wife, Saucy Girl #2.

"Sounds good."

Gina headed back toward the kitchen, checking on the other occupied tables as she walked past. I picked up my iced tea and drank half the glass in one gulp. When I set it down, I noticed Elliott watching me.

"What?"

"I was serious before."

"About?"

"You're grumpy. You need to–"

"Do not say it."

He laughed.

"You're just proving my point."

This isn't the first time Elliott has commented on my sex life. Or rather, lack of one.

"Why are you so obsessed with my sex life?"

"Because, like I said, you're grumpy." He took a long sip

of soda, for what I'm sure was a dramatic pause, then continued. "And your bad mood messes with my zen vibe."

"You wouldn't know a zen vibe if it bit you in the ass."

He rested his elbows on the table and leaned closer.

"Again, you're proving my point."

Thankfully Gina returned with the antipasto. She must have sensed something going on between Elliott and me, because she placed everything on the table and left without saying a word.

I filled my plate, making sure to take extra meat, cheese, and olives. Especially olives because they're Elliott's favorite.

"Jamie, you can't isolate yourself."

"*Isolate*?"

I shoved a forkful of salad into my mouth wanting to kick myself for engaging. Elliott is a fixer and I don't want to be fixed. Hell, I don't *need* to be fixed.

"Yes, you do need to be fixed."

I frowned as I finished chewing, trying to figure out if I said that last sentence out loud. Elliott rolled his eyes.

"I've known you your whole life. You don't think I know exactly what you're going to say before you say it?"

"My life is fine the way it is. I don't need to get laid or whatever else it is you're concocting in your mind."

He held up his hands in a *no offense* gesture then groaned when Italian dressing dripped from his fork down his arm. If that had happened when we were kids, he would have licked it off, but now he picked up his napkin and wiped it away. Then he surprised the hell out of me by changing the subject. Not that I'm complaining.

"So do you think everything will be done by the time the class starts Sunday?"

"*Everything* might be tough, but we'll definitely have the

main part of the studio ready. After the second coat of paint dries, I'll get the floor trim and lights installed. While I'm doing that, you can start painting the dressing room and bathroom."

I ignored his sour face and listed everything else on my to-do list. I'd just finished when Gina approached carrying our pie.

"Half fresh tomato, half meat lovers." She set it on the table between us and my mouth watered as I inhaled the garlicky goodness. "I'll bring you some refills. Need anything else?"

"No, this looks great."

"Thanks Gina," Elliott added.

We both stared at the pizza, knowing better than to reach for a slice while it's fresh out of the oven.

"So if I help finish painting, do you think you can help me out with something?"

I wanted to point out that I'm *helping* him renovate *his* studio, but that would only delay him telling me what he wants.

"What's that?"

"I could use an extra person to help out with the certification classes."

I was shaking my head before he even finished the sentence.

"Oh come on," he whined. "I'd only really need you for Sunday and Monday. There are less people for the level three and four certifications."

"Elliott–"

"Norine has a family emergency out of town and can't make it. It's nothing you can't handle. I swear. Mostly just spotting the students. I'll take care of the rest." His mouth curled into a wide, toothy smile. "Please."

"I'm not qualified."

"I literally just need someone there to spot and observe."

I reached for a slice of meat lovers and took a big bite, ignoring Elliott's pleading stare as I chewed. He knows I'm in-between projects right now so there's no reason I can't help. And if I say no, he'll just drive me crazy until I say yes.

"Fine, but just Sunday and Monday."

"Thank you."

"But understand that you owe me."

"Maybe a room full of sexy women will be payment enough."

I shoved the rest of my slice into my mouth before I could tell him that's more of a deterrent than an incentive.

GET YOUR COPY HERE: HTTPS://GENI.US/IAXDQS

Chapter 1

Sophie

"I can't believe you're here!" Throwing my arms around Eve, I tugged her through the front door and into a tight hug. "I've missed you so much."

"Don't mind us," Anjannette said. "We'll just stand out here and freeze."

Still holding onto Eve, I backed into the house, allowing Anjannette and Keera to enter. I pulled back just far enough to see her face.

"I can't believe you're here," I said again.

"I know. It kind of feels like I've been away forever."

"That's because you have."

She chuckled.

"It's only been a few months."

"Eight," I said. "It's been *eight* months."

"I know. I planned on being here for Christmas, but then my whole family decided to come out to Seaside for the holidays."

"I get it, but I really missed you."

"Don't mind Keera and me over here," Anjannette said from the dining room. "We'll just amuse ourselves and eat all this food."

I released Eve then we both walked over to the dining room. Anjanette and Keera had brought pizza and wings and set the table with the paper plates and napkins the restaurant provided.

"Nice of you to join us."

I grabbed a slice and looked over at Anjannette.

"There's no need to be dramatic," I said.

"Dramatic?" she placed her hand against her chest *dramatically*. "Moi?"

"Always."

She shrugged, then took a big bite of pizza.

"So tell us everything that's been going on with you and Max," Keera said to Eve.

"You act like you don't grill me for details during our Zoom calls."

"It's not the same." Keera shook her head. "We like you in the same room."

"Not that we're not thrilled that you've found true love out there on the left coast," Anjannette added.

Keera pointed between Eve and me with a chicken wing.

"And if one of you doesn't write *that* story, I'm gonna scream."

Eve's trip to visit her aunt in Seaside, Oregon last

summer resulted in her falling in love with the local handyman and moving to the idyllic coastal town. The fact that said handyman is not only nine years younger but also happens to be the former child star of one of the hottest TV shows from the last decade makes their story that much more interesting.

I spread my arms out wide and pointed at myself.

"Not to brag, but I am the one who predicted her life would imitate a Hallmark Channel movie before she went out there."

"Then write the damn story," Keera said.

"I think Eve needs to do it. It would be great for marketing."

"Yeah, but that would be icky. Even though it'd be fiction, readers would think I'd opened the door to our bedroom."

"You say that like it's a bad thing."

Keera bobbed her eyebrows and Eve threw a crumpled napkin at her forehead.

"Besides, Max and I are old news. Keera and Simon are the new kids on the block. Not to mention the fact that Anjannette and Leo are engaged and planning a huge wedding."

"Even if we just included Leo's immediate family, the wedding would be huge."

I finished two slices and a handful of wings as Anjannette filled Eve in on her latest adventures in wedding planning. I half listened since I've already heard some of it. Leo is from a big Greek family and they're trying to get married without having to rent an arena to fit all the guests.

It's funny, when I started taking pole dance lessons at the studio, Anjannette had sworn off men, Keera was healing a broken heart by dating *dick band-aids*...her words, not mine...

and Eve and I were both newly divorced. Now the three of them are in healthy, happy relationships.

"But enough about me," Anjannette said. "Sophie is the one living the *Sex and the City* life. Hearing about that is more interesting than listening to my guest list woes."

"I told you guys that I'm done with the dating scene."

"Yeah, but we didn't think you were serious," Keera said.

"Oh, I'm serious."

"You were having fun *exploring*." Eve said. "Did something happen?"

She looked alarmed as she asked that question and I quickly reassured her.

"No, it just stopped being fun."

"I get that," Keera said. "It turns into a grind after a while."

I finished my wine and set the glass down, keeping my fingers wrapped around the stem.

"Rob was the only person I had sex with and after the divorce, I was kind of like a kid in a candy store. But after a while, I wasn't enjoying it anymore." I circled my pointer finger around the rim of the glass as I collected my thoughts. "I even checked out those BDSM clubs, but it only made me realize that lifestyle isn't for me." I shifted my gaze between the three of them. "So I'm done with dating. I'm better off on my own."

Keera and Anjannette shared a look then burst out laughing.

"Famous last words," Anjannette said.

"Yeah, you know both of us took a man break and then Leo walked into her life and I rediscovered Simon in a whole new way."

I shook my head.

"I was married for twenty years. I'm not looking for a relationship."

They all nodded, but the looks on their faces said I'd eat those last words as soon as the perfect man walked into my life. Especially Eve's since she said the same thing last year.

"I'm serious," I said. "Been there, done that, and have written many books."

"Good one," Keera said.

"Thanks, I pride myself on my wordmanship." I popped the last bite of crust into my mouth and chewed, debating on whether I want to share my next thought. As I swallowed, I decided I did. "There is one thing I'd love that I didn't get while I was *exploring*."

"What's that?" Eve asked.

"Amazing sex." Three sets of rounded eyes just stared at me. "What?"

"You didn't get that with *any* of the guys you were with?" Anjannette asked.

"You say *any* as if I banged the whole third fleet," I said. "I was pretty selective about who I spent time with and I only had sex with the few guys that made me tingly in all the right places." I shook my head. "Unfortunately, none of them lived up to those tingles."

Keera leaned forward, resting her elbow against the table, and held up one finger.

"Not one?"

"Nope." I sighed. "A couple were better than the others, and one had a few moves I enjoyed. But honestly, not one of them gave me an orgasm better than I can give myself."

"Damn."

Anjannette punctuated that single word by picking up her glass and finishing her wine in one gulp.

"And the thing is...how do you know? They walk the

walk and talk the talk, and then..." I made a raspberry sound and gave a thumb's down.

"The struggle is real, my friend. Honestly, I don't think I've ever been with a guy who didn't need training." A slow smile spread across Anjannette's face. "Well, except for Leo."

"Which is why you're putting a ring on it," I said. "But I'm not lying when I say I don't want anything serious." I took in a breath and let it out. "You know what I really want?"

"I think this is going to be good," Eve said in a stage whisper then leaned toward me, and smirked. "What do you want?"

"I want a man to take me out to a nice dinner, bring me home, fuck me hard...preferably with multiple mind-blowing orgasms...then go away until the next week. A true friend with benefits. Hell, we can even skip the *friends* part as long as the chemistry is there and he satisfies the afore-mentioned requirements." I held out my hands. "You'd think I'd be every man's fantasy, wouldn't you?"

"You'd think," Anjannette said.

"That sounds logical to me," Keera said. "But Granny Vi always said that at a certain point, men either want a nurse or purse. Meaning they want a woman to take care of them or to support them."

"I am so using that in my next book," Eve said. "I'll give Granny Vi full credit, of course."

"She'll be thrilled."

"Maybe I need to have Granny Vi pick a man for me. She's proven her ability to predict dick size. Maybe she can take one look and know if a guy is a dud or a stud in the sack."

"I'll ask if she wants to be your wing woman."

"In the meantime, until I can find a man who will give me what I can't give myself, I'll stay solo."

****

Jamie

"You could help, you know."

"But you're doing such a great job all by yourself," Elliot said from his perch on the black velvet sofa across the room. "I don't want to mess up your system."

"My *system* is putting paint on the roller and pushing it against the wall."

"You're better at it than I am."

I climbed down the portable scaffolding, unlocked the wheels, and pushed it to the other side of the wall.

"I did all the trim. All you need to do is get off your ass, pick up a roller, and start painting."

Out of the corner of my eye, I saw him stick his tongue out at me as he stood. I shook my head and leaned down to lock the wheels, then climbed back up.

"Know what I think?"

"Not really, but I'm sure you'll tell me anyway."

"You need to get laid," he said. "That's why you're cranky."

"I'm not cranky."

"Yeah you are. You're cranky and grumpy."

"I'm not. I just want to finish renovating *your* studio. I need you to help if you want it ready for your training class."

"It's not my fault I'm not good at this stuff."

"Spare me," I said. "Growing up, we worked side-by-side with your dad doing *this stuff*."

"It's just not my thing." He looked up at me and smiled. "That's what I have you for."

I shook my head and went back to the task at hand. I'm starving and I want to finish this first coat before stopping for lunch.

Behind me, I heard Elliott shuffling around. A quick glance over my shoulder confirmed that he'd finally started to paint.

If I'm being totally honest, when he asked me to help him renovate the pole studio, I didn't really expect him to pitch in. I just like to bust his ass.

"Do you like this color?"

Squeezing the handle of my roller until my knuckles turned white, I ignored the question and kept painting, hoping Elliott would let it go. But history has taught me that he wouldn't, and history is rarely wrong.

"Jamie. Jame. Jamie."

Taking in a calming breath, I slowly let it out and turned around.

"There's no need to say my name three times. You sound like Sheldon from the *Big Bang Theory*."

"You weren't answering."

"What do you want?"

"Do you like this color?"

"Yeah, it looks great."

He scrunched his nose.

"You think?"

"I do, which is why I said it."

Backing up to the middle of the room, he turned in a circle.

"I don't know." He gestured with the roller. "It looks kind of...blah."

"You're just used to the walls being Pepto Bismol pink."

"Hmmm."

Cocking his head to the side, he studied the wall he'd just painted.

There's no way in hell I'm repainting. With these high ceilings, the trim took forever and doing the top half has been a pain in the ass.

"Don't start second-guessing your choices. The burgundy and gold look good, especially with the exposed brick wall."

Elliott narrowed his eyes.

"The colors are *copper red* and *anjou pear*."

"Whatever. You're looking at one coat with the sun and all the lights bouncing off it."

He shrugged.

"Maybe."

He'd been planning this renovation for months and it took him longer to pick out the paint than make any other decision. I figured I'd have to do more convincing, but surprisingly, he went back to the task at hand.

With both of us working, the walls were completely covered within a half hour. It took another ten minutes to get cleaned up and within fifteen we were walking through the front door of Saucy Girls Pizza.

Saucy Girl #1, Gina Romano, waved as we sat at our favorite table in the corner. She approached a minute later and set a Diet Coke in front of Elliott and handed me an unsweetened iced tea. Being a regular has its privileges.

"Having the usual?" she asked.

"Yes," I said. "And I'll have an antipasto salad, too."

"We'll take two plates with that salad," Elliott said.

Normally I'd tell him I'm not sharing, but the salad in question is big enough to feed a family of four, and I don't want to watch him pout.

"Got it. Cara is just finishing up a big takeout order, but

she'll get on this asap," she said, referring to her wife, Saucy Girl #2.

"Sounds good."

Gina headed back toward the kitchen, checking on the other occupied tables as she walked past. I picked up my iced tea and drank half the glass in one gulp. When I set it down, I noticed Elliott watching me.

"What?"

"I was serious before."

"About?"

"You're grumpy. You need to–"

"Do not say it."

He laughed.

"You're just proving my point."

This isn't the first time Elliott has commented on my sex life. Or rather, lack of one.

"Why are you so obsessed with my sex life?"

"Because, like I said, you're grumpy." He took a long sip of soda, for what I'm sure was a dramatic pause, then continued. "And your bad mood messes with my zen vibe."

"You wouldn't know a zen vibe if it bit you in the ass."

He rested his elbows on the table and leaned closer.

"Again, you're proving my point."

Thankfully Gina returned with the antipasto. She must have sensed something going on between Elliott and me, because she placed everything on the table and left without saying a word.

I filled my plate, making sure to take extra meat, cheese, and olives. Especially olives because they're Elliott's favorite.

"Jamie, you can't isolate yourself."

"*Isolate?*"

I shoved a forkful of salad into my mouth wanting to

kick myself for engaging. Elliott is a fixer and I don't want to be fixed. Hell, I don't *need* to be fixed.

"Yes, you do need to be fixed."

I frowned as I finished chewing, trying to figure out if I said that last sentence out loud. Elliott rolled his eyes.

"I've known you your whole life. You don't think I know exactly what you're going to say before you say it?"

"My life is fine the way it is. I don't need to get laid or whatever else it is you're concocting in your mind."

He held up his hands in a *no offense* gesture then groaned when Italian dressing dripped from his fork down his arm. If that had happened when we were kids, he would have licked it off, but now he picked up his napkin and wiped it away. Then he surprised the hell out of me by changing the subject. Not that I'm complaining.

"So do you think everything will be done by the time the class starts Sunday?"

"*Everything* might be tough, but we'll definitely have the main part of the studio ready. After the second coat of paint dries, I'll get the floor trim and lights installed. While I'm doing that, you can start painting the dressing room and bathroom."

I ignored his sour face and listed everything else on my to-do list. I'd just finished when Gina approached carrying our pie.

"Half fresh tomato, half meat lovers." She set it on the table between us and my mouth watered as I inhaled the garlicky goodness. "I'll bring you some refills. Need anything else?"

"No, this looks great."

"Thanks Gina," Elliott added.

We both stared at the pizza, knowing better than to reach for a slice while it's fresh out of the oven.

"So if I help finish painting, do you think you can help me out with something?"

I wanted to point out that I'm *helping* him renovate *his* studio, but that would only delay him telling me what he wants.

"What's that?"

"I could use an extra person to help out with the certification classes."

I was shaking my head before he even finished the sentence.

"Oh come on," he whined. "I'd only really need you for Sunday and Monday. There are less people for the level three and four certifications."

"Elliott–"

"Norine has a family emergency out of town and can't make it. It's nothing you can't handle. I swear. Mostly just spotting the students. I'll take care of the rest." His mouth curled into a wide, toothy smile. "Please."

"I'm not qualified."

"I literally just need someone there to spot and observe."

I reached for a slice of meat lovers and took a big bite, ignoring Elliott's pleading stare as I chewed. He knows I'm in-between projects right now so there's no reason I can't help. And if I say no, he'll just drive me crazy until I say yes.

"Fine, but just Sunday and Monday."

"Thank you."

"But understand that you owe me."

"Maybe a room full of sexy women will be payment enough."

I shoved the rest of my slice into my mouth before I could tell him that's more of a deterrent than an incentive.

ABOUT THE AUTHOR

As a tween, Tina Gallagher and her best friend would create happily ever afters for their favorite soap opera couples. Eventually, the soap operas lost their appeal, but the writing never did.

Before living her dream as a full-time author, she worked a spectrum of jobs ranging from baking and cake decorating to marketing and project management.

In between creating memorable characters, traveling, and taking pole dance lessons, Tina enjoys spending time with her two grown children and Golden Irish named Thea.